The Man with
the Silver Eyes

by the same author

THE BUFFALO KNIFE

WILDERNESS JOURNEY

WINTER DANGER

TOMAHAWKS AND TROUBLE

DAVY CROCKETT'S EARTHQUAKE

THE LONE HUNT

FLAMING ARROWS

DANIEL BOONE'S ECHO

THE PERILOUS ROAD

ANDY JACKSON'S WATER WELL

THE FAR FRONTIER

THE SPOOKY THING

THE YEAR OF THE BLOODY SEVENS

THE NO-NAME MAN OF THE MOUNTAIN

TRAIL THROUGH DANGER

WESTWARD ADVENTURE
The True Stories of Six Pioneers

THE OLD WILDERNESS ROAD
An American Journey

THE WILDERNESS TATTOO
A Narrative of Juan Ortiz

The Man with the Silver Eyes

WILLIAM O. STEELE

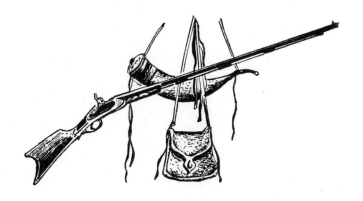

Harcourt Brace Jovanovich

New York and London

Title page drawing
by Paul Galdone
from *Winter Danger*
by William O. Steele

Printed in the United States of America

First edition

B C D E F G H I J K

Library of Congress Cataloging in Publication Data

Steele, William O   1917–
The man with the silver eyes.

SUMMARY: Until he learns the reason for the
arrangement, a young Cherokee boy has mixed emotions
about living for a year with a white man.
[1. Cherokee Indians—Fiction.   2. Indians
of North America—Fiction]   I. Title.
PZ7.S8148Man   [Fic]   76-18850
ISBN 0-15-251720-0

For my uncle

LEE DOZIER

who took me hunting and fishing
and to burlesque

And for my aunt

CAMILLE DOZIER

who put up with our wanderings
and fed us on our return

The Man with
the Silver Eyes

Chapter 1

A NIGHT-EVIL was after him. Talatu was sure of it. He stopped under a tree and looked about, clutching his load of firewood. He saw nothing in the twilight. But the sharp barbs of terror racing along his spine told him a night-evil was near.

Suddenly the loud scream of an owl came from the tree overhead. Fear gripped him. It *was* a night-evil hunting him.

A purple flame dropped from among the leaves and flickered round and round him. He was so frightened that he hurled the wood at the blob of light. It disappeared, and immediately afterward the owl flew softly off. Talatu did not wait even to pick up the firewood, but raced home as fast as he could.

He was lucky to escape without harm. Night-evils could cast spells on the unwary, young or old, and cause diseases. They took the shapes of owls or ravens. Sometimes they darted about the darkness as lights or flames.

He was out of breath when he reached his grandmother's dwelling. He was safe, and for that he was grateful. And he would not say a word about what had happened to his grandmother or great-uncle. They would worry. After this, he would be careful not to venture outside after dark.

But for a long time he lay awake, his thoughts on what had happened.

The following morning Talatu, the Cricket, sat outside his house thinking about the flying terror that had lain in wait for him the night before. He was as brave as any Cherokee boy not yet old enough to take the warpath. Still, it took more than courage to face a night-evil; it took the strong medicine and help of a conjurer. There was no conjurer in the town of Chota. That was one of the reasons it was very dangerous to live here.

Only the Cherokee old ones, like Talatu's grandmother and her brother, Old Coat, lived in the town now. That was why so many night-evils lurked among the empty houses and roamed the streets. They were here to steal from the old and the weak, suck the very being from their bodies and add it to their own lives so that they could continue to live on and on.

Old Coat, with a stool in his hand, came hobbling out of the hut. He placed it on the ground beside his nephew and slowly eased himself down. Talatu was filled with sadness for his great-uncle. Once Old Coat had been a great warrior and head man over several Cherokee towns. Now the Intruder lived in his knees, making them stiff and painful, and he moved with difficulty.

"Uncle, when do you think my mother will come for me?" the boy asked.

Old Coat sniffed the air a moment before he replied, "Are you eager to leave us old people?"

"No, Uncle," Talatu answered quickly. But he was. There was no protection against the night-evils, and it made him uneasy.

"It is not that I want to leave, Uncle," Talatu went on. "You have taught me much about my people. You have been generous with your wisdom. But—"

Old Coat turned toward him. "But you are eleven years old, and it is the way of the young to leap about when they can and not stay in one place." He paused and smiled. "Especially one called Cricket," he added.

"My mother was in my thoughts when I awoke this morning," the boy explained. "And Dragging Canoe's new town of Running Water. It is beyond the Pot That Boils in the Water."

Old Coat nodded and said, "So I have been told."

"Would you like to see it?" asked Talatu. "You and Grandmother might visit there."

"New towns are all alike," the old man said with a grunt. "I have seen many in my lifetime." He rubbed his knees. "The sun is a friend."

They sat in silence. Talatu brushed his long, loose hair from his eyes and gazed toward the Twenty-four Mountains, rising high and fog-shrouded in the east. His uncle had told him often of the myth of the Great Vulture who with its wings had shaped those peaks

5

and valleys for the Cherokee. The mountains still belonged to his people. He would like to hunt there before he left Chota, just once, but there was no one to take him.

At last Old Coat broke the silence. "Perhaps your mother will come for you when she has a new warrior in the house," he said.

His mother's choice of a husband meant little to Talatu's future. Talatu belonged to the Wolf Clan of his mother, just as she belonged to the Wolf Clan of her mother. A father, a new husband for his mother, would have no influence over him. Wolf did not marry Wolf, and only members of the Wolf Clan could teach and advise young Talatu.

"What does matter," thought the worried Cricket, "is that I might have to live in Chota through the winter moons." He would not like that. Besides night-evils, there were the pale-faced Americans. They could never be trusted. And Chota was so close to their dwellings at Watauga. It would be nothing for them to swoop down on horseback. He did not care to run from them a third time.

"Uncle, do you count on peace, living so near the unegas?" Talatu asked. "Will they not raid again as they did a few years ago?"

He had been eight then and living here in Chota. Cherokee scouts told of a white army approaching the town, and Talatu and his family had fled south with other people to join Dragging Canoe in his towns along Chickamauga Creek. A few months ago, this past spring, another army had raided the Chicka-mauga towns, and once more he and his family had fled. This time the Americans had killed the Cricket's father, but there was no time for sadness and mourning, for his mother had to get Talatu away. Alone, and brave as always, she guided them through the woods back to Chota.

When his mother left Chota to go to the town of Running Water, she had told Talatu he must stay here to hunt for the old ones. Old Coat was no longer able to bring home meat and depended on others to provide. Since there were not too many hunters in Chota, the pots were seldom full.

Twice Talatu had seen the white men bring terror and destruction. Twice he had run from them and had felt the pain of it twisting through him. A third time—he could not think about it.

"No, it is Dragging Canoe they will raid again, no matter where he has his towns," Old Coat replied thoughtfully. "Many of us older Cherokee leaders did not want the Canoe to declare war against the Americans. We wanted the Cherokee to do as did the Creeks and not take up the war ax for either side."

"But the British unegas are our friends," the Cricket argued. "They have helped us since time out of mind, my mother's brothers tell me. The Canoe had to hold fast to the chain of friendship with them and fight the Americans."

"It is a strange war, British brother fighting against American brother," the old man mused. "We would never do that—not the Cherokee—no matter how we hated one another. Still, it is the Canoe's right, as it is the right of every Cherokee, to do as he pleases."

Old Coat paused and seized his nephew's arm. "Listen," he whispered, "my sister's voice is as clear and sweet as when she led the dance songs in her youth."

Talatu listened to Neeroree stirring about in the dwelling. It was a love song she sang. Talatu had heard his mother sing it often, but never with such feeling, the way his grandmother sang it.

> *"No one is ever lonely when with me.*
> *I am very handsome.*
> *I shall certainly never become blue. . . ."*

Neeroree hummed a bit, then ended:

> *"No one is ever lonely when with me.*
> *Your soul has come into the very center of my soul,*
> *Never to turn away."*

In the quiet that followed, Old Coat stared dreamy-eyed toward the mountains. He sighed several times. Did he wish he was young again and in love, Talatu wondered. Perhaps not. Perhaps he was simply remembering. To grow old was part of life. Old Coat looked forward to another world; he did not long for a time past. At last his uncle roused himself and turned again to the Cricket. "Neeroree fills her days with love songs and good thoughts toward others," he said. "And I have made my peace with all unegas, both British and American. Before I go to the Darkening Land, I want to live my last years on earth with quiet thoughts, not bloody tomahawks and enemy scalps."

Talatu did not argue. It would be disrespectful. His great-uncle was revered as head of the family. But Old Coat's beliefs were not ones that he and his mother and his young uncles shared. They believed as did Dragging Canoe that the British were friends and could be trusted, but the Americans never! Talatu was sorry that the family was so split. This was one more destructive thing the American unegas had done to the Cherokee.

Old Coat added, "The Americans are too many. Already they have surrounded the Cherokee. Peace, little Cricket, that is the only way the Cherokee as a people can survive. Learn to live with the unegas."

"Yes, Uncle." Talatu nodded. But he wondered how it was possible to live with unegas who cheated you out of your hunting lands, who burned your towns and crops. People who could do such things . . .

Inside the hut his grandmother scraped the brass pot with a metal spoon. "Cricket," Neeroree called. "The stew is gone. You must kill us some meat today."

"It is a fine day for hunting, Grandmother," the boy answered. "No wind, and I know where deer will be feeding."

Talatu liked to hunt with Old Coat's trade gun. He

had managed to keep meat in their dwelling, with enough left over to share with neighbors and friends. "But I never believed my mother would leave me here so many moons," he thought.

Suddenly Old Coat leaned forward, staring toward the river. "One crosses," he said, shading his eyes with his hand. "A white man." He jumped to his feet.

Talatu had never seen his great-uncle move so quickly. Who could this unega be to make the old man forget the pain in his knees? A white official of importance? Or one with evil words and lying papers to say that Chota belonged now to the Americans? He watched curiously, but troubled, as the white man approached leading a packhorse. A trader, he thought, a silly unega who believed these old people had many skins to trade for his rattling pots and easily bent spoons.

Old Coat spoke without taking his eyes from the white man. "Go visit with Swallow. I think he has something to show you."

"Very well," Talatu answered. But he wished first to see the white man, coming slowly toward them. "He is thin and bony as the great blue heron," Talatu observed to himself. The Cricket wanted to see his face, but it was hidden under a wide-brimmed hat.

"Talatu!" Old Coat spoke sharply. "Be gone!"

Talatu was startled. Was it something so important that Swallow had to show him? Or was it that his great-uncle did not wish him to have a close look at this unega? He stared at Old Coat and opened his mouth to protest. But a boy did not argue with his elders.

Reluctantly, he began to walk away toward Swallow's house. His feet dragged in the dust, and once he glanced furtively over his shoulder.

What he saw made him stumble. Old Coat and the scrawny stranger stood looking at each other for a moment, and then they reached forward in the embrace of old friends.

Chapter 2

TALATU threaded his way between the clumps of weeds and burrs and new pine saplings. At the next dwelling he stopped. No one lived there. The inhabitants had fled long ago and not returned. Slabs of the bark roof had blown off, exposing the supporting poles underneath. He watched idly as a woodpecker dug into a pole with its bill, sending a steady stream of rotten chips raining down.

He would wait here, he decided. He would not go looking for Swallow. Something strange was taking place in his own house. He would stay and watch and discover what he could. He did not wish to disobey Old Coat, but he was too worried to leave.

He squatted in the grass under a peach tree, watching his grandmother's dwelling. Snatches of laughter floated through the morning air. When had he last heard Old Coat chuckle like that? Then the unega appeared and untied the bundles on the packsaddle and took them inside. He heard Neeroree suck in her breath with a great "Oooo."

He rose to move closer so that he might hear what she had to say. But before he could take a step, Old

Coat walked out the doorway and, seeing him, beckoned. The unega appeared behind the old man and grabbed the lead line as his horse edged toward a nearby clump of grass.

Talatu approached the two men with a mysterious feeling of foreboding. His uncle spoke unega words in a careful tone. "Talatu . . . this . . . is . . . Ben-a-min Shinn."

The boy looked up at the tall figure, but he could see no more of the man's face than he had earlier. It was squeezed into a tight, dark knot under the limp brim of the hat. And if the unega had eyes, Talatu could not tell. He took a dislike to Shinn at once. No man should hide his eyes in shadow as this one did. A warrior's being lay revealed in his eyes—his strength and his fears, his pride or his disgrace. Perhaps the pale one had a great shame to hide.

"Howdy, Talatu," he said in a harsh, rough voice.

The boy took the bony hand offered him. There was no strength in it. He shook the hand once and quickly let it go.

Old Coat guided his nephew inside, leaving the unega standing in the sun. It was dark in the hut, but enough light came through the doorway and the smokehole in the roof for Talatu to see sugar loaves and bags of food about the hearth. And spread across Neeroree's bed was a bright red calico dress and a white man's heavy coat with bright buttons.

Then Talatu saw something that made him shrink with cold and fright, and it was all he could do to keep from trembling. His grandmother was bundling together his blanket and few possessions.

"They have sold me to this unega for all these goods," he thought in panic. "I am to be a white man's slave."

Old Coat sat on his stool and motioned the boy down beside him. "Little Cricket, this Shinn walks a lonely path," he said. "You shall keep him company till the next Green Corn Feast."

It was true then. The unega had bought him. Talatu squatted there beside his uncle, stunned and unbelieving. Belong to a white man! It was cruel. Rage and bitterness filled his head, and he almost cried out at the unfairness of Old Coat. With great difficulty he fought back his fury and forced himself to show nothing and to breathe in a calm fashion.

At last he spoke. "I had hoped to live soon with my mother in Dragging Canoe's town," he said quietly. It would never do to speak in anger. That would be disrespectful, and Old Coat would scold him for letting his feelings rule his tongue.

His uncle nodded. "You have told me many times. You shall go when the time comes, if you wish."

"There will be no one to hunt for you," the boy pointed out.

"We will manage," Old Coat replied. "Someone will share with us."

"I will be living among my enemies," Talatu went on quickly.

"Are you afraid?" the old man asked.

Talatu was startled. Fear had no place in his thoughts where whites were concerned—he who was soon to become the Canoe's warrior. But he saw what Old Coat had in mind. Talatu would be one lone Cherokee boy among white strangers. He would be on his own whatever happened. It was not for the weakhearted.

"Afraid? Perhaps—a little," he stammered. "More so if this American is a rogue."

"He is no rogue," answered Old Coat. "His gods tell him to treat everyone kindly—Indian or white."

"I am to be his slave?" asked the boy.

"No," replied Old Coat. "You go as my nephew."

Still, Talatu could not imagine even a peace-loving unega making this strange request. Why had he ridden a hundred miles to ask for him? No Cherokee warrior ever rode to the Watauga villages and asked for a white boy to come and live with him. Why did his uncle give in to this unega so easily and quickly?

"Some other boy could do as well," he said, almost sullenly.

"How many boys have you seen in the Overhill Towns here along the Little Tennessee?" asked his uncle and added sadly, "Only the old, the sick, and those weary in heart and thought live here now."

He picked up a glass bottle and poured oil into his palm and rubbed it into his knee.

It was eel oil and sweet fern, Talatu knew. He had

prepared it under his uncle's direction. Old Coat said it helped, but Talatu noticed that he moved more slowly and painfully than ever these days.

"And, Talatu," continued Old Coat, "your ears are open to the white man's words."

"That is true," the boy said, nodding.

He listened with care and understood most of the white man's tongue. His mother spoke the language well, as did some of his uncles. The Canoe had many mixed bloods—children of Indian mothers and white fathers—who could speak the language of both their parents with ease. But Talatu had to admit his mouth did not always shape the white man's words easily.

"Shinn—he knows I hate white men?" the boy asked. "That I will fight against the Wataugans when I am of age?"

"He knows, for I have told him," admitted Old Coat. "But he walks a blue path of loneliness. His wife and young son were killed many, many months ago— and scalped!"

His uncle spoke the last words sharply. Talatu understood. Dragging Canoe's warriors had done this.

"Will he not hate me then?" the boy wanted to know.

"No, his thoughts are sweet," Old Coat replied. "His religion is strong with peace and love for all."

"He is a strange man then," Talatu thought. The Cherokee believed in revenge—an injury for an injury, a death for a death. If a warrior harmed you or killed one of your clan, it was only right to retaliate in the same way against that warrior and his clan. Talatu believed that the unegas felt the same way.

He looked at his grandmother. She had finished packing all his belongings. Now she squatted by the hearth. Her face was calm and neither happy nor sad. What had been decided was what was to be.

"Then I must go," he thought. There was no hope. He must do as the old ones thought best. Talatu reached for his moccasins and slipped into them and tied the thongs around his ankles. Old Coat's word was law.

He stood and strapped his steel knife and sheath on the belt that held up his breechclout. He tied his hair together at the back of his head.

Old Coat rose slowly to his feet. "Come," he said. "It is time." He lumbered through the doorway.

Talatu followed. After the dark of the hut, the bright October sun hurt his eyes. He stood blinking for a moment. The white man gazed at him a long moment, but neither of them spoke.

His grandmother came up beside him with his possessions wrapped in his blanket and tied with thongs. Shinn took the bundle and placed it on the pack saddle.

Talatu turned and hugged his grandmother, burying his face in the wrinkled folds of her neck. "Nahwun-yu-ga-i, Grandmother," he murmured.

She held him close for a moment and whispered in his ear, "Go then, Talatu. Go and keep the Red Man deep in your heart." Then she thrust him away.

The boy smiled at her. She had always been more sensitive to his feelings than her brother. She knew he was leaving with anger churning inside him, and she was worried. She sent him away in the protection of the Red Man, Thunder, the special friend of all Cherokee.

"Do not worry, Grandmother," Talatu whispered back, "Thunder will keep me safe." He hoped this was true. Still he did not want Neeroree to worry about him.

Talatu embraced his uncle, then shook hands with him as befits one warrior to another. "I will pray, Uncle," he said. "I will be a good Cherokee and not shame you before the unegas. I will ask the spirits' help until I may return. I will not—" He broke off. He did not truly understand what was happening or what he would or would not do.

"We must be off, lad." The white man spoke for the first time. Talatu did not reply. Shinn turned to the old people. "I'm mightily obliged. You'll hear from me in time. And from this Cricket." He led the horse away.

"May the path home be straight and free of danger," said Old Coat in his slow way.

The dwelling sat on a rise. Talatu followed down the slope and past the garden his mother had once so carefully tended. It was a tangle of broken sunflower stalks and nettles. Beyond was the house where he had grown up believing he would never have to leave it. The roof had fallen in, and brier vines grew up the front wall and snaked through the doorway. This was the work of the unegas, and it filled him with black rage. How could he go to live among them?

They crossed the edge of the weed-cluttered square and walked on through ramshackle houses and wasted gardens and then under wild plum and apple trees growing beside the winter house belonging to one of Talatu's young uncles. Low and earth-covered, it was now the home of a fat groundhog. The animal crouched in the doorway and watched them.

At the river's edge he turned to look back, but Old Coat was hobbling back inside the dwelling, helped by Neeroree.

"Already I am forgotten," Talatu thought gloomily.

He waded the shallow stream and on the far bank paused for one last look at Chota. It was a desolate and dreary view. A stranger coming on Chota now would never be able to tell that it had once been the strongest town in the Cherokee Nation and its head men listened to and respected in distant places. Only the earth-covered council house was untouched. Once the life-beat of the town and nation, it seemed to Talatu to stand as proud and as undaunted as ever.

"Chota, Great Echota . . . sacred town among the mountains . . ."

It was all he remembered of the priest's chant. Chota had never meant so much to him as now. Already he was homesick.

With a sigh he turned away and moved north along

the ancient war path. He should be brave as any warrior facing uncertain days among the enemy. But he was *not* brave. He feared what lay ahead.

Yet in his heart he feared more what lay behind him. In his heart he knew that it was not the coat and the calico that had made Old Coat and Neeroree send him away. There was another reason. What it was he did not know. But whatever it was, it was dark and secret and mysterious—and it made him afraid.

Chapter 3

SHINN walked at a good pace for a white man, jerking on the horse's line and glancing neither left nor right. Talatu had to trot to keep up with those long-striding legs. The path was hard-packed and wide, so tree limbs and bushes did not crowd the travelers or brush across their faces and arms.

The Great Indian War Path was old and much used. Cherokee went northward on it to raid the unegas of Watauga and Virginia. And white armies had ridden south over it to drive away the Cherokee of the Overhill Towns along the Little Tennessee River. Traders, hunters, scouts of northern Indian tribes and those from southern America had walked this wilderness highway since time out of mind.

But Talatu knew that never before had the path been used to send an Indian boy to live among the white skins. Never before had it seen such strange companions as the two of them now. Never before had a young member of the Wolf Clan been so betrayed by his family.

He was furious at all of them, especially at his

mother and Old Coat. Now he saw why she had never come to Chota to take him away.

"My thoughts are black enough to scare the Thunder Man himself," thought the Cricket.

Yet he realized that there was nothing he could do about his plight, only accept it and try to behave so as not to disgrace Old Coat and the Wolf Clan. Were he to bring shame to them, their scorn would be terrible. If his young uncles were here, they would not feel sorry for him at all. How many times had they told him a Cherokee warrior took whatever fate brought him, whether torture at the hands of an enemy or a victory dance in the town square.

"A warrior's life-path is filled with danger and hardship," they had said, "and he must learn to accept whatever awaits him."

Behind them a great crashing noise made the horse shy. Talatu glanced back to see two does cross the path in graceful bounds and disappear into the undergrowth with white tails flashing. Shinn never bothered to look around; he only yelled something at the pack animal and kept pumping his long legs.

The Cricket had been so filled with anger that he had taken no notice of Shinn's horse. Now he saw that its movements were as lithe and graceful as a deer's—the white man's deer. The horse was another of the unega's possessions that had proved helpful to the Cherokee. Many elders of the nation held that Cherokee should return to the simpler days of their forefathers and once again use clay bowls, shell spoons, and bows and arrows. Talatu's young uncles thought otherwise—take the white man's guns and metal knives and tomahawks and horses and use them to kill those who traded them to the Cherokee, take them and drive the whites away from Cherokee lands forever. And Talatu agreed.

Still, of all the white man's store, a horse was the hardest thing to come by. Traders brought guns and powder, ruffled shirts and hoes, knives and bangles to the Cherokee towns to trade—but never a horse. The best way to get a horse was to steal it.

How Talatu longed for the time when he would own an animal as fine and shapely as Shinn's. On his first war raid against the unegas, he would capture a horse, one that would make his young uncles proud of him. Let others bring home scalps. A horse first.

It seemed to him that it took forever to grow up and be a warrior.

He quickened his pace, pursuing his thoughts of the happy days ahead as a young warrior with Dragging Canoe, and almost stepped on Shinn. The unega was flat on his stomach drinking from a small stream that bubbled across the path and away down a little hillside.

Shinn rose and pointed to the muddy bank opposite. "A bear done beat us here," he said. "A big old fat one ready for a winter's sleep." He smacked his lips. "Wish he'd tote his meat up to my cabin door."

He crossed the stream and walked on. Talatu

dropped down and drank. Under the water a salamander crawled across a rock on stubby legs. It was
the one Old Coat called a rainmaker because it came
out of streams in dry weather and wailed and wailed
to bring down rain. The boy thought it strange that
such a tiny creature had that power. Some of the
greatest of Cherokee conjurers had trouble making
rain fall when dry weather destroyed the corn.

He lay for a moment watching the salamander and
the many crayfish shuffling about in their underwater
world. Suddenly something struck him in the back.
He leaped to his feet, startled. But it was only a
sweet gum ball that a little gold and black bird had
knocked loose as it hopped about in the tree overhead, eating the winged seeds from the spiny balls.

He did not know how long he had lain there. Leaping the stream, he set out. He had not gone far before
he came on the horse, tied to a sapling beside the path
and cropping grass.

Talatu peered in among the trees on both sides of
the trail, but there was no sign of Shinn. The unega
could not be hunting, for he had no gun, only a knife.
Talatu squatted, and the horse raised its head to stare
at him. There was green froth on its lips. The beast
suddenly snorted, and the foam flew straight into the
boy's face.

The Cricket laughed and wiped off the foam.
"When I escape from Shinn," he said aloud, "I'll take
you with me. You would like the Canoe's town and
the easy, happy life there."

The day-traveler dropped lower in the sky. The boy wondered if something had happened to Shinn. Perhaps a bear had killed him, or he had fallen over a bluff. Then the unega appeared suddenly out of the dimness of the trees. He had his hat filled with chestnuts and beechnuts.

"Reckon we can use these for our supper meal," he remarked. "They'll go good with the bread and baked apples your grandmother packed for us."

Talatu nodded and almost cried out in astonishment. He was seeing Shinn's face and eyes for the first time. The unega had the palest eyes he had ever seen—gray, and not much darker than the whites around them.

"They are silver glass-bead eyes," the boy told himself. Who could see with eyes like that? No wonder the man wore his hat low on his forehead. Who would want others to see such no-good eyes?

Shinn wedged his hat among the bundles on the packsaddle, and they started off again. The white man began to whistle, and the faster he whistled, the faster he walked. Talatu let him rush on ahead. He was tired. Why should he rush?

Fat clouds floated overhead; in the light of sunset they were as red as the maple leaves lining the path. Soon Shinn would stop for the night. The path wound back and forth across a stream. It was too wide to jump. The Cricket took off his moccasins and tied their thongs together to hang about his neck. He hated to walk in soppy footgear.

Suddenly he rounded a bend in the path and saw figures far ahead, moving about a horse. Was it Shinn's horse? Who were those others? He walked slowly and softly, trying hard to see who they were and what they were doing. Then, in a sudden brilliant sundown flare, he saw quite clearly—there were three Cherokee, and they had Shinn tied to a tree.

Chapter 4

TALATU stood quietly and watched as the warriors cut the bundles loose from the packsaddle. One of the strangers emptied Shinn's hat and clapped it on his head. It was too small and sat there loosely. He began to chant, slapping his bare thighs in rhythm and dancing around his companions.

"Ha ayi ha, ho yi ho," he sang, twisting his face to one side in a terrible grimace.

His companions laughed and Talatu grinned, for the warrior's face resembled a mask worn in a Cherokee dance that made fun of the unegas. But the dancer tired and snatched the hat from his head and cut it into strips and threw it into the bushes.

Another knelt on the ground and went through Shinn's bundle. The Cricket's eyes turned toward the unega and found him watching the three indifferently. Talatu certainly did not care what took place. He would not stop the warriors from taking any booty they might find. And if they wanted to kill and scalp Shinn, the Cricket did not see that it was his duty to try to stop them from that either. It would be an easy way to rid himself of the white skin. His great-uncle could not accuse him of deserting Shinn. How could one boy keep three warriors, tall and strong of arm, from acting as they wished?

Out of Shinn's quilt tumbled a worn shirt, a goose quill sharpened to make a pen, a leather bottle filled with liniment. All of it was cast aside. Now the same Cherokee began to open Talatu's pack. There was nothing in his blanket that they could possibly want, the boy thought, and yet he resented a little having them handle his things. Suddenly the searcher held up a thong from which dangled a curious-looking stone.

Talatu sucked in his breath in astonishment. It was Old Coat's amulet of stone. What was it doing in his bundle?

"That is mine!" he cried out.

The three warriors glanced around, startled. Shinn said nothing. The Cherokee relaxed when they saw Cricket.

"Asiyu, little brother," the searcher called to him.

The boy returned the greeting and came and took the stone from the warrior's hands. "I am Talatu. This belongs to my great-uncle, Old Coat," he explained. "He would think ill of me if I lost it."

"Old Coat of Chota?" inquired the warrior.

The boy nodded.

"Then I know your uncles in Running Water Town," spoke up the one who had danced wearing Shinn's hat. "Why have I not seen you with them?"

"I have been with Old Coat since the Chickamauga

towns were destroyed," Talatu said. "Are you from the Canoe's new town?"

"No, from Long Island Town," the dancer replied. "Why are you with this miserable one with the empty eyes?" He gestured toward Shinn.

Talatu was too ashamed to tell the truth. They would chide him and ridicule Old Coat for being friends with this unega. Live among the white skins! What a mad thing to do! He could hear them saying that and laughing at his old uncle and making ugly remarks about him.

"I was guiding him to the Nolichucky unegas," he lied.

"Ah," the searcher exclaimed. He picked up his rifle as did the other two.

They were leaving, thought Talatu in surprise. They were going without harming Shinn at all. He was disappointed. It would be so easy for them to take this scalp. It was not like the Canoe's followers.

As he had trotted behind Shinn, hating him more with each step, he had sent many prayers upward to Thunder. He had asked the Red Man to hurl lightning and strike Shinn dead, or to make a tree fall on the paleskin. He had prayed for any kind of help at all. Talatu had been sure these three strangers had been sent by the Red Man. And now they were going away, leaving Shinn unharmed. Even his hat could perhaps be repaired.

"Wait," pleaded the Cricket. "Before you go, kill the unega."

The hat dancer laughed. "Such a bloodthirsty young warrior. Your uncles will be proud of you when I tell them."

"Why do you not kill him?" the boy demanded.

The three warriors looked at him in disapproval. It was not right that he should question them. Still they answered.

"We leave him for you to kill, if that is to be his fate," the dancer said. He stepped over to Shinn and cut his bonds. "Bring his scalp to Long Island Town, and we will dance with you."

"For my part," said the third warrior, "I do not want to interfere with Old Coat's plans. If he wants this white one to reach the Nolichucky, then let him reach there. Old Coat would not like us to interfere. And there might be clan trouble for me if I killed the unega." He began to run, loping down the path.

"Let your eyes be open among the unegas," the dancer warned. "Step with care, little brother." He raced after the leader, and the other Cherokee followed.

Talatu watched until they disappeared. He had almost been free.

He still clutched his uncle's good-luck charm. It was a flat stone, gray and rough and big as the boy's hand. Embedded in it was another kind of stone, light-colored, long and pointed, and very smooth to the touch. There was not another like it in the Cherokee Nation.

Why was it in his blanket, he wondered. He knew

the answer. Old Coat had put it there to guard Talatu. He had sent his most powerful and precious magic to watch over the Cricket. Though Old Coat was an old man with a bent back and crooked knees, he had thought Talatu's need greater than his own. He had sent the stone as a message of love and hope.

"My path shines bright," Talatu whispered to himself.

Shinn stood rubbing his red-marked wrists. "I got to thank ye kindly, for I reckon you must have saved my life," he said. "Leastways you talked enough with them to save a body's life."

The Cricket stared into the glass-bead eyes. Surely the man must know that Talatu had wanted him killed. Could those pale eyes not see what had happened? Perhaps not—few of the unegas could see or hear or smell very well—unlike the Cherokee.

Talatu was relieved. Thunder *had* helped him. For as long as Shinn believed he had saved him, the Cricket benefited. He slipped the stone's thong over his head.

"What is that thing around your neck?" Shinn asked curiously.

"A gorget—a rock I found—" Talatu lied.

The boy did not want to tell what it was nor how the Old Coat came to have it. He knew the story by heart, for his uncle had told him many times how he found the stone while hiding from a war party of Shawnee. How he had held it in his hands for a whole day and prayed for help. How a terrible storm had sent the Shawnee running and saved his life.

His great-uncle had kept the wonder-working stone, and it had helped him many times through danger and trouble. It meant a great deal to Talatu that Old Coat had sent it with him to help and protect. He was not worthy of such a sacrifice. He had never done anything to prove himself worthy.

Shinn went looking for his hat. He held it up and thrust his fingers through the slits in the crown and wiggled them at the boy. "You saved my worthless carcass," he said, "but you let my old hat die an awful death."

Shinn threw back his head and laughed. He clapped the hat on his head and added, "Wearing a dead hat never hurt a body." And he laughed again.

He gathered up their scattered possessions. He brushed the dirt from the bread and wrapped it and the nuts in his quilt. The baked apples he left lying in the dust. Tying all their things on the horse, he said, "I made sure they'd take Shucky anyway if they didn't kill me. You're a powerful talker. There's a mite of light left. Let's get on." He picked up the lead line and walked off along the path.

Talatu slipped on his moccasins and followed. The stone slid back and forth across his bare chest with each step.

"I will endure this," he whispered to himself. "I will be worthy. Old Coat will not have made a useless sacrifice of his stone." Through the shadows he went steadily on.

Chapter 5

LATE on the following day the two made their way over a rough path. It was the hardest traveling they had done since leaving Chota. Bushes slapped at them, rocks tripped them. Still Shinn hurried. At the bottom of a small bluff, he brought the horse to a stop.

"Home," he said and began to take the bundles from the horse's back.

Talatu stared about the clearing. There was little to see—piles of logs and stacks of flat rocks and a white man's cabin with the walls only three logs high. Were they going to sleep inside those walls, penned in like hogs?

Shinn threw the bundles on the ground beside an iron cooking pot.

"Hungry, ain't you?" he asked and added, "Me too. Hungry enough to eat knotholes and beg for more."

Talatu turned away. There was nothing to say. Shinn knew they had eaten little all day.

"I got a haunch of deer back there under the bluff," the man went on. "See can you find it whilst I hobble

Shucky down by the creek. Old feller's as hungry and tired as us."

Talatu stumbled through dimness under the rock ledge. There was a pool of water here, and around it were casks and buckets. At the rear of the rock room, the meat dangled by a thong attached to the ceiling. He untied it, sniffing hungrily at its ripe odor.

Shinn had lit a fire. Talatu handed the venison to the man, who placed it on a large flat boulder and held out his hand. "The loan of your knife, Cricket," he said. "Your friends done took mine."

Shinn cut off slices of the dark meat and threw them into a skillet with bits of fat.

"I'll fry us some up right quick," he told the boy.

Holding the vessel over the flames, he turned the meat with the knife as it cooked. Talatu could not take his eyes from the venison. Never had he smelled anything so good. Shinn picked up a wooden trencher and blew the dust from it and gave it to the boy. Then he raked all the meat into the plate.

Talatu ate. The trencher was empty in no time, and Shinn filled it again. The boy nodded his thanks and went on eating. Shinn fried some of the meat for himself. Then he sliced the rest into the pot.

"I got some beans and cornmeal somewhere," he explained. "I'll put them in and let this stew the night, and our breakfast meal'll be ready and waiting in the morning."

He cleaned Talatu's knife on the leg of his breeches and handed it back. "You can sleep over there under them hemlocks," he said. "I reckon you ain't caring how hard your bed is tonight."

Talatu crawled in under the drooping limbs and wrapped himself in his woolen blanket. He could hear the nearby stream, the voices of crickets, and one last katydid. The fire blazed up, and the flames lit the cracked and pockmarked bluff. He clutched his great-uncle's wonder stone in his fist. His unega life had begun.

It was quiet, and the night shadows still clung to trees and rocks when Talatu pushed through the hemlock branches the following morning. He headed for the creek, and fog came up to meet him, swirling about him in damp ribbons. He shed his breechclout and waded into the water. Its coldness numbed him for a moment, but as he splashed about, the blood leaped through his body. His skin tingled, and a warmth spread over him. He got out feeling light-headed and refreshed.

Tying his flap back on, he walked slowly through the trees. He was a little fearful of what the day might bring and of what Shinn might ask him to do. Had he been brought here to be a slave—to carry rocks and drag trees and help in building a cabin? He groaned at the thought of wasting his days in such a useless way. Yet, what else was there for him to do here?

Shinn busied himself about the fire, adding wood and tasting the stew steaming in the pot. "Good morning," he called. "Eat when you've a mind to." Then he disappeared into the rock room.

The Cricket was hungry, but first he wanted to comb his hair. From his bundle he took a trader's comb made of horn and raked it through his hair until the dampness was gone. He wished for some bear's oil to comb into his hair. He knew his grandmother would have given him some if there had been any in the dwelling.

Perhaps Shinn had some. But on second thought, that seemed unlikely. The paleskin did not care about keeping himself clean. He had not been out of his breeches and shirt since their meeting in Chota. Why should he comb and oil his hair? It did not matter how tangled his hair became, for he wore his hat all the time and had even slept in it on the path. White skins were strange—and very dirty!

Talatu took the long black hairs from the teeth of the comb and threw them in the fire. He returned the comb to his bundle. Back at the fire, he helped himself to stew. Squatting, he picked out pieces of the soft venison with his fingers and popped them into his mouth. Then he scooped up the beans and lumps of cornmeal with his hand until the trencher was empty. It was as good as any stew his grandmother had fed him, but never would he tell Shinn this.

As he ate a second helping, the man came toward him with a rifle in his hand. Talatu could see it was a fine gun, a much better one than the smooth-bore weapons British traders sold his people for deerskins. Only one of his young uncles had a rifle, and Talatu had never shot it. He pretended not to look.

Shinn placed the gun on the flat boulder behind the boy. "That there is a dandy shooting piece, and I call her Miss Never," he said.

Talatu did not know what the man was talking about. He wondered if all unegas called their guns Miss Never.

"Ain't nothing that rifle can't do," Shinn went on. "I reckon she's smart enough to go a-hunting deer by herself, did I let her. But I'd a heap rather have Miss Never hunt with you, Cricket."

Talatu almost dropped the trencher. He glanced up suspiciously into those silver glass-bead eyes, but he could not tell whether Shinn was serious. Surely, Talatu thought, he had not understood the man's words. Surely, he would not be trusted with a rifle. Why, he could kill Shinn any time he wanted to with this weapon or shoot any paleskin in Watauga. The man must be teasing him.

"I ain't the best of hunters," Shinn explained. " 'Sides, I got my hands full finishing this here cabin afore cold weather. You meat the pot for us, Cricket."

The boy put down his trencher and went over to the rifle and stared at it for a moment, marveling at its slim beauty. He wiped his hand on his clout and picked the rifle up and placed the curve of the butt to his shoulder. He sighted down the barrel. Though it was longer and heavier than Old Coat's gun, Talatu knew he would have no trouble hunting with it.

"Fine gun." The boy nodded. "Damn good!"

Still, he was cautious. Shinn was trying to make friends with him, trying to win him over to white man's ways. Shinn knew it would be difficult for Talatu to keep away from such a beautiful weapon. Once he began shooting Shinn's gun and bringing in game, they would cease to be enemies. They would be brothers.

He placed the gun back on top of the boulder. "No—might break," he said. "Be bad—you have broke gun."

Shinn looked at him steadily. "You can mend a broke rifle," he told the boy. "I ain't brought you here to starve. You can help if you do some hunting. I aim to get this cabin roofed before hard frost. You can help some with that. But most you can help by getting us some meat."

A crow called nearby, and another answered from the top of the bluff. Talatu glanced upward. The sun was just touching the tops of pines. The day would be warm and bright. He wished he was at home in Chota.

Shinn went to the fire and picked up a pewter mug lying on its side in the cold ashes and filled it from the pot. Some of the stew dripped into his beard as he sipped.

"I got a heap too much to do," Shinn went on. "I

ain't owned this land but a couple of months. I got no proper furnishings. Got my stones yonder, but there ain't enough to build a chimley. I ain't even begun to frow out my oak shingles."

His eyes swept over the clearing and under the cliff. He shook his head. "I need help bad," he said. "You hunt and half the skins'll be yours, and you can swap them for a rifle of your own."

Talatu's heart beat fast; the blood pounded in his head. A rifle of his own! To return to Old Coat and his young uncles with such a weapon as Shinn's would make them grind their teeth in envy. He was only eleven years old. And a rifle of his own! It was unbelievable. He would hunt for this paleskin. He would remember why. He would hunt in order to earn a rifle for himself—not in order to become a white man's friend.

"I hunt." He nodded gravely.

"Only trouble is, I ain't got a lick of powder," Shinn responded. "Storekeeper's saving me some. We'll go after the powder. We'll get me a knife, too."

Shinn got an empty leather bag for the powder, and they set out walking. As the morning passed, the sun burned away the fog, and the bright October day was hot. The trees began to thin, and soon their way led across meadows and along fields. Talatu glimpsed a cabin here and there back from the path. Once a group of men and boys felling trees shouted and waved to them.

At last they passed beside a dwelling where a woman pounded corn in a hollow log with a thick pestle. She nodded shyly when Shinn spoke, but the Cricket saw her eyes tighten at the sight of him. He straightened his breechclout and held his head a little higher. He was a Cherokee, one of the Principal People, a member of the Wolf Clan, and she was nothing—a poor, dirty unega! He would walk with dignity. Let the paleskins see that the Cherokee were a people who knew how to behave among strangers.

Behind the cabin was a smaller structure of logs.

"McCaul's store," Shinn told the boy. "Old man ain't been at storekeeping long and ain't got much to sell. But he's got powder and knives."

Outside the open doorway several white men sat about on chunks of wood. Their rifles leaned against the building in a row behind them. A man in a fringed shirt stood apart, slouching against a tree. He was whittling, slicing long, curly parings from a board. He saw them first and began to grin. Talatu had never seen a man who looked so much like an opossum—rows of crooked animal teeth in a chinless mouth—a unega opossum.

"Looky yonder what's a-coming," the man sang out.

The others looked around. Talatu saw their eyes slide past Shinn and rest on him. There was no friendliness in those faces. He would not let them frighten him. But their eyes were speaking to him, telling him in blunt words of their hatred of Indians.

"Help me, Thunder," he prayed and moved forward at Shinn's side. He had not imagined it would be so difficult, to be among his enemies and not show fear. He felt their rifles pointed at his chest, though the weapons still leaned against the wall. It was all he could do to keep from turning and racing away.

"Howdy," Shinn called out pleasantly, but no one answered. "McCaul here? I come for some powder. Ain't got a lick to hunt with."

"Hunting scalps, might you be?" asked a man with a bald head.

"I wouldn't have no luck with you, would I?" Shinn asked.

They came up to the whittler. Talatu stared straight ahead. As he moved past the whittler, the man reached out and with a quick flick of his knife sliced through the belt that held Talatu's breechclout. The flap fell to the ground around his feet and almost tripped him before he could stop. Panic gripped him.

"Oh, my soul alive!" guffawed the whittler. "Ain't that something to see." He roared with laughter, and the others joined him.

Talatu stared down at his nakedness in horrified shame. Snatching up his clout, he rushed away with his enemies' laughter loud in his ears.

Chapter 6

"TALATU!" shouted Shinn. "Cricket!"

The boy did not stop. Talatu wanted to get as far as possible from all unegas. He ran hard, blindly. Limbs of trees and bushes slashed his face and body, briers ripped his legs, but he did not stop or cry out. He welcomed the hurts and stings. It was like having a priest scratch his body with a gar-tooth comb to purify him. And he desperately needed to be cleansed of the white men.

At last he stopped and leaned against a tree, breathing hard. There were rivulets of blood on his chest and legs from the cuts. He fingered the wounds on his face and wiped away the taste of blood from his lips. But the scourging had failed. Rage and shame and hurt burned in his throat.

He knotted his belt together and tied his clout in place. Nakedness was commonplace among his people. Children ran the town streets bare, and the Cricket had not been long in clothes himself. Everyone bathed in the rivers. But he knew it was not the white man's custom. He knew that what had been done to him had been done to humiliate him, to make him comical, to show the unegas' disgust for him.

He set out, pushing slowly through the undergrowth toward Shinn's home place. He would leave, he decided, pack his possessions and head for Chota before Shinn came back. He would tell Old Coat how he tried to face the unegas. And his great-uncle would share in the boy's anger.

Would he not?

The old man would sit and smoke thoughtfully while his nephew told him what had happened. Then, when Talatu had finished, Old Coat would point out in sharp, blunt words how childish such behavior was. He would remind the boy that no Cherokee warrior allowed his feelings and his fears to take charge of his actions—not among his own kind and certainly not among strangers.

Old Coat would never excuse him. He would go on to repeat over and over that Talatu should not have run. He should have tied his clout back in place and faced the unegas' stares and jeers with proud dignity. A member of the Wolf Clan and a Cherokee did not allow others to goad him into cowardliness, did not act like a four-year-old.

"He will talk on and on," the Cricket moaned aloud, "and chide me and tell me what was right to do and what not. I know he will say I disgraced him and brought shame to Shinn also. And the lucky charm—what use could it be to one so disgraced?"

43

Talatu ground his teeth until his jaws ached. He saw that he was caught helplessly between what Old Coat expected of him and what Shinn wanted from him. There was no running away, no hope of pity from his great-uncle. He could only stay here in Watauga and accept what came his way as best he could.

By noon he reached the clearing, tired and dejected. His face and body burned from cuts and scratches. He searched in the rock room and found a gourd of deer tallow. He dug his fingers into it and smeared the grease over his wounds. That helped on the outside, but not on the inside. Inwardly he was raw and seared, and nothing would help him. Only vengeance—only the sight of all white men standing helpless and shamed as he had stood.

The spring water rippling among the rocks at the entrance to the room had been dammed. He watched a cloud of butterflies settle on the pool's bank in the sunlight and swarm over the damp sand—tiny blue-gray ones and brown-and-orange-winged ones and some palest yellow.

What were they after, crawling about like that, he wondered.

He squatted to watch and, disturbed, the tiny creatures rose as one and floated round and round him. His eyes were dazzled by rings of tilting, whirling colors. As if commanded, the throng settled back on the damp bank, to rise a moment later and hover around him again. For a long time Talatu stayed there, enjoying the sunlight shimmering on their never-still wings and their feathery dance along the pool's rim. His troubles were forgotten.

Suddenly he heard Shinn, singing loudly. He moved to the hearthstones and helped himself to stew. He did not want the unega to see him playing childlike among butterflies.

Shinn splashed across the creek and gave a shout. "Talatu, I got that powder."

He crossed the clearing and laid the bag of powder on the flat-topped rock by the fire. Turning, he handed Cricket his new knife. "See what you think of it whilst I get my rifle out of hiding," he said and moved off into the rock room.

Talatu glanced quickly at the knife and then laid it beside the powder. It was a knife like any knife brought into the Cherokee Nation by traders. Did Shinn expect him to praise it?

At least the white skin had had the courtesy not to mention what had happened at the store. That was the right thing to do.

Shinn returned and laid the rifle on the rock with the powder. Then he began to pour the black grains from the bag into his powder horn. He was careful not to spill any, though he talked all the while.

"I've told folks in these parts you was coming to live with me," he said. "They marked me a Tory for it. Oh, they were all under the bedstead when brains were passed out. Let a man do the least little thing they wouldn't do, and he's all kinds of a fool and a son of Satan."

He held the horn up to the light. It had been scraped thin so that the level of powder inside was plain to see. Pouring a bit more, he stoppered the horn and turned to face the boy.

"That there whittling feller, he's Felty Tyce," Shinn went on. "He likes me like he likes a rattlesnake. He got drunk in a tavern once and knocked down the little maid carrying the mugs. I give evidence against him, and they put him in the stocks. Folks made a heap of fun of him. Tyce don't like being mocked. He's hated me since, and he'll do most anything to see if I'll get in a fight with him. Tyce knows right well I ain't given to fighting. In my younger days, when I was a heap better Quaker than I am now, I got used to such folks. I've forgot a heap of what I learned at meeting. But I still can't believe fighting's good for anything." He paused. "Cherokee don't hold with that, I reckon."

He picked up the rifle, shot bag, and powder horn and came to where the boy squatted.

Talatu had hardly been listening, for his eyes and thoughts were on the rifle. He almost snatched it from Shinn, so anxious was he to shoot it.

"I shoot?" he asked, reaching for the gun, unable to hold back any longer.

Shinn grinned and placed the paraphernalia in the boy's hands. "You shoot," he answered. "Come on. I got a tree over yonder across the clearing I practice on."

Talatu followed eagerly. Tonight he would fast.

Then at dusk he would cleanse himself with water and prayers in the stream below. As his people so often did, he would ask help of the stream, the Long Man.

And tomorrow! Tomorrow he would have as much luck in hunting as did Kanati, the first Cherokee hunter, in the age-old tales his great-uncle told. He would bring home much game and many skins. All over Watauga the unegas would hear and know that no man anywhere could shoot more swiftly and truly than Talatu, the Cricket!

Chapter 7

IN THE early-morning darkness Talatu lay awake, going over a list in his mind.

He had performed all the rituals necessary for a successful hunt. He had gone to water and asked the Long Man's help; he had prayed to Fire and to Kanati, owner of all game; he had smeared ashes from the fire on his chest; and he was fasting. There was nothing else. He had remembered everything Old Coat had taught him long ago. Today it was very important that these ceremonies should be carried out exactly. So he went carefully over the list, even though he had done all these things many times before.

In the clearing the crickets had ceased their chattering back and forth to one another. Nothing stirred in the woods. The predawn world was hushed; it seemed to hold its breath, as if everything waited and watched for Talatu to begin his hunt.

Suddenly a wolf cried nearby, a long, throaty howl. Talatu sat up, startled. Prickles raced down his back. Excitement pounded in his chest. A clan brother called him to the hunt. The moment had arrived, and he must be on his way.

He reached up for his uncle's amulet, which hung by its thong from a low hemlock limb. He held it in both his hands for a moment, and its strength flowed through him. He crawled out of his blanket and stood. He would not go through the woods naked today. His chest and arms, when he moved, were stiff under the dried blood, as if strips of his skin had been pulled together and tightly sewn. The coarse woolen breeches and shirt would give him protection.

He dressed quickly. Then he slipped the strap attached to the shot pouch and powder horn over his shoulder. Pulling the gun from its canvas sheath, Talatu headed across the clearing.

Out of the dimness loomed the stripped white target tree. As he passed, he ran his hand over the roughness of the trunk where his bullets had shredded the bark in practice shots.

"There ain't a thing wrong with your shooting eye," Shinn had declared yesterday. "You done good. You and Miss Never make a dandy team."

Talatu remembered the words with a glow of pride, though he had been careful at the time not to show his pleasure. He did not want to become friendly with Shinn. However, there had been no praise for the slow way in which he had loaded the weapon. At least the white man had not lied.

Before, the Cricket had not used a linen patch and ramrod. All he had to do to load Old Coat's trade gun was to pour powder down the barrel and drop a lead ball after it. One slap of the stock and the bullet rested on the powder, ready to fire. Now he had to wrap a cloth patch around the ball and use a ramrod to force them both all the way down the long barrel to the powder. He was awkward now, but with practice his motions would become swift and smooth.

Rising above the clearing was the tree-covered slope of a mountain. To the east, along its lower levels, Shinn had told him there was a stretch of burned-over woods where deer often browsed on sprouts and suckers of the charred trees.

The unega was not awake this morning; his snores were loud as the boy passed his bed. Last night Shinn had stayed away from Talatu when he performed his ritual.

The white man had not questioned the boy about his actions or followed him to the creek or even spoken to him. He had behaved almost as if he knew what Cricket was doing. It would be strange if he did. Few unegas knew about the Cherokee sacred practices, much less paid them any heed. Perhaps Old Coat had told Shinn.

Talatu left the clearing and hurried toward the east. He wanted to be at the burned woods by sunrise. The ground was rocky among the trees, and he stumbled about, banging the gun stock on trunks and rocks. He stopped and ran his fingers over the wood. There was a scratch across the stock.

He wondered what Shinn would say about that. It could not be helped. Anyway, the gun would shoot just as true as when it was unscratched.

50

Farther on, the trees thinned, and he found himself in a tangle of vines and low bushes. He had trouble pushing through with the weapon, for it was as long as he was tall and caught in everything, no matter how careful he was. Trade guns were short and easy to maneuver in thick growth. He had not realized how difficult it would be to handle a long rifle in the woods.

The sunlight touched the mountain rim over him and began to drop slowly down the slope. Now there was more light among the trees and walking was easier. Squirrels scuttled in fallen beech leaves as they searched for nuts. If he had been after squirrel meat, there would not be a squirrel in sight. He hastened on. In the distance a quail, seeking its covey, gave a sad "quoi-eeee" cry of anxiety.

By sunrise Talatu had reached the edge of the burned area. The remains of the forest rose up against the dawn sky in strange, thin shapes. A faint odor of charred wood hung in the air, though he could see that the trees had been destroyed some time ago. Little new pines and sedge grass sprouted among the fallen timber and stumps, and here and there red clusters of sumac leaves and berries brightened the dismal blackness.

The soft wind followed him. He would have to work his way to the top of the burned woods in order to be upwind of the deer grazing in the open. He slipped quietly up the slope.

Talatu pulled back a branch of laurel. Nothing

stirred among the new growth, but across the ruined woods a movement caught his eye. At first all he could make out was a tiny sliding of light and shade. But the longer he stared, the more he saw. Bit by bit, a black nose emerged from the shadows, the streak of light became a white throat, pointed leaves were clearly two alert ears, and then—he sucked in his breath—those branches were antlers curling upward out of a buck's head.

The gods had been good to him!

The Cricket let the laurel branch ease back into place and with wildly thumping heart began to pour powder into the rifle. He rammed home the ball and patch, sprinkled a bit of the black grains into the firing pan, and the gun was cocked and ready to shoot.

Resting the weapon on a thick limb, he peered out again. The buck was gone. He scanned each shrub, but it was useless. Nothing was there. He slipped from the undergrowth and, crouching as much as he could with the great rifle, ran forward and hid behind an outcropping of rock.

He knew what he would have to do. He would have to call deer to him, the way his people had always done since ancient times.

In a low voice he sang:

"O Deer, you stand close by the tree,
 You sweeten your saliva with acorns.
 Now you are standing near.
 You have come where your food rests on the ground."

He waited a little and then chanted, "Listen, O Ancient White! O Kanati! Bring the deer close." Then he sang the song once more.

Three does came slowly browsing among the new growth. Every so often one would raise her head and sniff the air, then return to feeding. He was disappointed that his song had not called forth the buck. Still, here was meat and a skin.

Slowly, slowly, Talatu brought the cocked gun up and rested it on top of the boulder. He aimed down the barrel at the nearest deer, taking his time and lining the sights right behind the foreleg. He held his breath and pulled the trigger.

There was a flash, and smoke rose up close to his eyes. He held steady a moment while the fire in the pan lit the powder in the barrel. The rifle roared; the butt bit into his shoulder. He stepped away from the rock, expecting to see the doe thrashing about on the ground. Instead, leaping over the fallen trees were three does, racing away with white tails raised. He had missed!

He groaned. "How could I miss? How? How?"

He could not understand how this could be. He had taken his time and held the gun steadily—he knew he had. Yet, he had missed. Missed a shot with this fine rifle, a shot that he would never have missed with Old Coat's gun. Had he made the gods angry in some way unknown to him? He could not believe it. He was bitterly disappointed, but he tried to cheer himself.

"The day has only begun," he repeated over and over. "There will be other chances. And the next time I will not miss."

Now there was nothing to do but go elsewhere and call up other deer. He reloaded his rifle and made his way between the gaunt trees and broken limbs. He sang the deer song softly to himself as his eyes swept over the slope below him.

He walked for some time before he spied another doe. From where he stood, the shot would have to enter at an angle behind the rib cage to the lungs to kill the doe. It was troublesome. He should try for an easier shot. He ducked down into the brush and crawled forward to get a side shot similar to his first one.

At last he stopped and peered from behind a stump. The doe stood with raised head, her ears pointed forward and wiggling. Something was disturbing her. Satisfied that there was no danger, she dropped her head and began to browse.

Talatu held the rifle against the side of the stump. Once again he aimed carefully behind the foreleg and just as carefully squeezed the trigger and fired. With the smoking gun he ran forward, sure he would find the dead deer. The doe was sailing off down the mountainside in great bounding leaps.

Perhaps he had only wounded the animal, and he would have to trail her. He searched the ground but found no sign of blood.

He had missed another sure shot at close range!

For a moment he stood there staring stupidly at the gun in his hands, unable to believe what had happened. He had said all the prayers for success. He had aimed with a steady hand. How could he have missed both times? He could not understand it. Unless—unless—

Shinn!

The unega did not wish the Cricket to hunt successfully. He did not want Talatu to have skins and furs.

The unega had cast a spell on the rifle so that, no matter how carefully Talatu aimed, the ball would miss the target every time. There would be no more hunting for the Cricket. He would hand over the gun to the unega without a word. Shinn would know his spell had worked.

Gloomily he walked across the burned-over clearing to its lower end, where the woods began. He pressed through the thick mat of orange sassafras trees and grape vines and stopped. It was dim among the tree butts, and he waited while his eyes adjusted to the soft light.

Suddenly he gave a start. Stretched out on the ground among the tree roots was a long, dark figure. He gripped the rifle, and his heart leaped wildly in his chest. It was Shinn, waiting here for him. He began to edge away, sure that those glass-bead eyes were fastened on him. He did not know what to expect from the man. He only knew he had to get away.

Then he stopped and said in a breath of relief, "It is a deer—a dead deer."

He went up to the animal and saw that it was a doe with blood on her lips and a bloody hole in her side. There was a white patch across her forehead—the same doe he had last shot at and thought he had missed. Yet here she was.

How had an animal so badly wounded been able to run this great distance? Was this more of Shinn's magic? Could he move dead animals around as he pleased, like chips of wood?

It had been a strange morning, and Talatu did not like it. It made him uneasy to think that Shinn might be a white man's conjurer. Certainly he was different from other unegas the boy had known. Did he have magic powers?

Talatu did not know what to believe. He wished Old Coat had told him more about this strange man, Shinn. If only Talatu knew why he was here—if only his uncle had spoken out about Shinn—

He would have to watch Shinn closely. Yet if the unega had the power to take the boy's soul and destroy him, there was little Talatu could do by himself to prevent it. It would take a Cherokee conjurer to fight Shinn's magic. And there was no conjurer here. Only a lone boy, friendless and fearful.

Dropping to his knees, knife in hand, he set to work skinning the deer. He dreaded returning to the cabin clearing, but he had no choice. He must go back, he must go back to whatever awaited him.

Chapter 8

THE WEATHER worsened. Days were cold and overcast, and storm winds stripped the leaves from the trees and bushes. In the winter-bare woods, Talatu went hunting. He found a deer runway and places where herds came regularly to feed on mast and crab apples and fallen persimmons. He hid at these spots and waited patiently, though the wind bit into his fingers and rain drizzled through his clothes.

Now he had two dressed deer hides, and five others soaked in the pool below the rock room waiting to be scraped. And strips of venison had been fire-smoked and stored below the bluff.

The mating season had commenced, and the bucks were fearless and wild. Once, while he was loading the rifle, he had been charged by a great buck and had barely managed to climb a tree and escape the sharp antlers. That, however, had been his only real trouble.

Shinn was too busy to do more than nod to him. No matter what the weather, he worked at splitting logs into floorboards from sunrise to dark, singing and whistling all the while. At night, he crawled into bed—hat, shoes, and clothes—too tired to undress or to talk much to the boy.

The Cricket had kept a careful eye on him. The unega had done nothing suspicious so far. Cherokee conjurers prayed and fasted and performed many rituals in using their magic power. Shinn had done none of these things. The work on the cabin took all his time. He carried rocks from the mountainside and, with the help of his horse, dragged logs from the woods.

Talatu was thankful to be let alone to do as he pleased. Perhaps it was Old Coat's talisman that protected him. Perhaps it was his prayers to the Ancient Red. He was safe for the time being, though he still did not know whether Shinn was a conjurer or a crazy white skin.

Certainly things had gone well for him since that first bad day of hunting. He was proud of what he had accomplished.

One morning, when Talatu finished breakfast, he picked up the rifle. A metal piece on the lock was loose; it had happened during yesterday's hunting. Shinn had forgotten to fix it. Talatu was disappointed that there would be no hunting for him today. Yet it was just as well that he stayed and dressed another skin. The day looked to be sunny, and the clearing was sure to warm up later. Working with a wet hide was difficult when his hands were stiff from the cold.

Shinn had peeled the bark from a log and wedged one end under some rocks. It slanted gently over the creek bank, and this was where Talatu scraped the skins. Taking a hide from the pool, he squeezed the water from it and threw it over the end of the log. He straddled the tree trunk and picked up his scraping tool, a wide blade with wooden handles at each end. He had no idea what the unegas used it for, but it made an excellent tool for cleaning hair and fat from the skins. He had to be careful not to scrape too hard, else the sharp blade would cut through the skin and ruin it.

Women usually dressed the skins, but as Old Coat had often told him, any Cherokee warrior who could not prepare his own skins for trade was worthless. His fingers were not as clever at the work as his mother's or his grandmother's, but he managed.

Shinn was splitting shingles from blocks of oak, stacking up the thin boards at a steady rate. As usual, he sang, and once the Cricket was sure he heard Shinn softly chanting a Cherokee song, one of Grandmother's favorites.

"Shinn could not know the song," Talatu told himself.

He had imagined the words were Cherokee because he missed hearing his own language. He was homesick and wished there was someone to talk to him. His friend, Swallow, who was never quiet and never serious—how it would cheer him if the Swallow were here with him.

Talatu pulled the scraper across the skin toward him. Wiping the hair from the blade, he reached out again. Overhead, a flicker drummed on a dead tree. Suddenly the bird flew up with an alarmed "Wicker, wicker, wicker!" And someone shouted from across the creek.

Shinn straightened up.

"Hellloooo, Shinn."

Strangers, thought Talatu. What could they want? He slid from the log, holding the deerskin and the scraper.

"All's well, Cricket," Shinn told him with a smile. "This is an old friend of mine—Guy Tilson. He told me he'd come over one day and give a hand with the cabin raising."

Talatu did not believe he would like Shinn's friend any better than he liked Shinn. He did not want to stay here all day scraping the skins while a unega watched him. He wished the rifle was mended. This would be a fine time to get away.

A man in leather breeches, stockings, and a loose coat walked into the clearing. He led a horse on which sat a woman with a basket in her lap. Behind the woman, holding on to her, was a small child.

"Guy!" cried Shinn, moving forward. "Welcome. You're a sight for sore eyes."

They shook hands, and Shinn moved up beside the horse and swept off his hat and bowed. "Mistress Tilson, your servant."

Mrs. Tilson kicked playfully at him with her foot. "I never knowed you had manners," she said. "And I never knowed you Quaker fellers took off your hat to us worldly folks."

"There's a heap about me that folks don't know about," said Shinn, laughing and slapping his hat back on his head. "And I take my hat off to you for bringing a basket of vittles. Me and Talatu ain't the best cooks. We're fair starved for something decent to eat. And I reckon you to be one of the best cooks hereabouts."

"And I reckon you to be a great fool liar," Mrs. Tilson retorted, but Talatu could see she was pleased at Shinn's remark.

Shinn lifted the child down and sent him off with a slap on the rear. He took the basket of food and set it carefully on the ground, then helped Mrs. Tilson down.

A second man followed shortly. He carried a sack and a rifle. Shinn turned and shook hands with him. "Adam Kirk, howdy-do."

Kirk's eyes swept over the unfinished cabin and the piles of logs and rocks. "You need help bad, I see," he said. "And quick. I don't like the feel of this here weather. This winter is fixing to be a jack dandy."

Shinn looked a little worried and pulled at his beard thoughtfully. "Sure hope you're wrong," he said.

A boy and girl came up and stood beside Kirk. They did not speak, staring at Talatu. The Cricket glanced away. They appeared to be about his age, sour-faced and contemptuous of him. He had never seen unega children before, and he wished he was not seeing them now. It was going to be a long day for him, he thought uneasily. He threw the skin over the log and resumed his scraping.

Suddenly Shinn said, "That there's my friend Talatu. That's the way the Cherokee say 'Cricket.' And he's lively as a cricket, too. Helps me a heap. Good with the rifle, and he's a-saving hides to get his own gun."

The boy poked his sister with an elbow, and they looked at each other slyly and giggled. Kirk spoke to them sharply. "Mind your manners or I'll take a hickory to your backsides."

"How do," they murmured.

Mrs. Tilson said, "Well, he looks like a good strong young 'un."

"Betsy couldn't come," Kirk added. "The two least 'uns got a sickly rash. But me and these young 'uns will help all we can."

He held up his sack. "Got some sweet taters, and I'll stick them in the ashes so they'll be hot for our dinner meal."

Mrs. Tilson put in proudly, "I brought turkey pasties. And cornbread with butter and some turnips."

"Oh, a real feast we'll have," exclaimed Shinn.

He looked pleased. Talatu found nothing wrong with the food they had been eating, but evidently the white skin had hungered for something else.

"That'll be a treat for the little savage," added Kirk.

Savage! Talatu bristled with rage. He had heard that word flung at his people by white traders. He knew its meaning. Cherokee were nothing but animals, cruel, filthy beasts. How he hated the whites!

He put down the scraper—his hands were shaking too much to work. At least Shinn never called him a savage.

He rearranged the skin over the log, taking his time and keeping an eye on the white people. But they ignored him now and set to work on the cabin. The woman and the children stuffed mud and moss and grass in the cracks between the lower logs, while the men added more logs to the top of the walls.

At noontime, the visitors gathered about the fire, and Shinn urged the Cricket to join them. Talatu was reluctant to be in their midst or to eat their food. But he was terribly hungry, and everyone pressed food on him.

He ate, and it was good. He especially enjoyed the sweet potatoes, for he had not tasted any recently. Before Chota was raided years back, the storage houses were filled with potatoes. But the invading white army had destroyed these houses as well as the corn cribs. It saddened him to think that the food his people had needed was wasted. That had been a hungry autumn for all of them after the destruction.

"Shinn," said Kirk, taking a potato out of the

ashes, "show my boy how to throw the tomahawk. He hones to know how. But I told him I was a farmer, not a fancy hatchet thrower. I'd be mighty much obliged was you to give him a lesson."

"Glad to," answered Shinn.

He and the white boy went off to the far edge of the clearing where Talatu had practiced with the rifle. The Cricket had never thought of Shinn as a warrior, but he could see that the unega used the tomahawk with skill. He himself had not yet learned to throw a tomahawk. His young uncles were fine marksmen. And he would let them teach him; he would never ask Shinn.

The moment Shinn left, Mrs. Tilson began to question Talatu about Indians.

"Is it true that a Cherokee man has to leave a deer haunch before a woman's doorway to be married to her?" she asked.

The boy understood, and he nodded that it was so.

"Humph!" exclaimed Tilson. "Heathenish."

"Do the Indians believe in the Devil?" the woman continued.

Again the Cricket nodded. Old Coat had never told him about the Devil. What unega thing was this?

"I knew they followed the Devil," said Kirk, and the other two nodded knowingly with him.

"Do the Cherokee," Mrs. Tilson wanted to know, "eat pieces of broiled flesh of white captives?"

Talatu quickly muttered "Yes." He did not want to try to explain anything in his stumbling unega words.

Let them believe what they wanted to believe since all white skins said Cherokee were savages.

Shinn returned with the boy, and before Mrs. Tilson could ask another question, he said, "Cricket, move Shucky over in that little meadow across the creek."

Talatu was glad to leave. He hurried to get the horse. He had heard more than enough stupid unega questions.

He hobbled the animal at the edge of the meadow and lingered, watching a little bird make a hole in a sweet shrub pod and eat the seeds. A single large cloud was overhead and darkened the meadow; then the sunlight came drifting back, and the tall grass glowed golden red again.

There was whispering near him. It was the two children. He tensed and turned. Was that a small white face among the undergrowth? Or there in the shadow of that tree? More whispering. Then a rock sailed out of the woods and hit him on the head.

He cried out, more in surprise than in pain. He glanced around warily. He would have to fight—he knew he would. He waited for the two to rush out of hiding at him. But the woods were quiet. Shucky came up behind him and pushed him gently. He stroked the animal's soft lips.

Nothing more happened. The horse began to browse. Talatu felt his head. The blow had not been hard, and the swelling was small and not even painful. The fight was over.

"Cowards!" he exclaimed aloud. "Two cowards!"

For the remainder of the afternoon, he wandered about, searching under rocks along the creek for salamanders and crawfish and following the tracks of raccoons and opossums along the muddy banks. When he heard the visitors leave before dark, he made his way back to the clearing.

"Oh, there you are, Cricket," Shinn remarked. "There's more turnips and more taters, if'n you're hungry."

"No," he replied and walked over to the scraping log. He stared for a moment in disbelief at the skin he had left there to finish scraping. A strip had been cut out of the middle of it. It was ruined! All his work had gone for nothing.

"Shinn!" he cried, holding up the skin in his hands. "See—no good!"

Shinn came and looked at the deer pelt. "Them two young 'uns," he said angrily. "Ruining a good hide. Somebody ought to give them a licking."

He took the skin from the Cricket. "I can make some whangs out of it," he went on. "Naught to be done about it now or about the meanness of some chaps. Their pa's a good man anyway."

"Man speak—say Talatu savage," the boy said angrily. "Not savage—not Talatu—them—unega much savage!"

He turned and ran to his bed before Shinn could say a word.

Chapter 9

TALATU slipped out of his warm bed the following morning and raced to the stream. The cold cut into him like a knife blade, and every breath scalded its way down his throat and burned through his chest. He broke the ice at the edge of the Long Person, splashed himself with water, and after a quick prayer headed for the fire.

He warmed himself and dressed. Then he combed his hair. By the time Shinn threw aside his blanket and sat up, it was snowing.

"Morning, Cricket." He yawned. He rubbed his eyes with his fists and stood, fully clothed and hatted.

Talatu nodded and helped himself to stew. Shinn never allowed the pot to be empty, so that they could eat whenever they were hungry. In this he was like the Cherokee, for they followed no set time for meals. Food was always ready on the hearth fire in each house.

Only a little snow fell. The sun suddenly slanted through the clouds, and the ice-filled air sparkled with tiny falling rainbows.

Shinn ate, and in between mouthfuls he talked.

"I don't recall that we ever had such cold and snow this early before. . . . Winter's going to be cold as a snake. . . . That there goose you killed the other day . . ." He stopped and sucked a sliver of meat from a bone and held it up for the boy to see. "Here's the breast bone, and you can see how thick it is and how white. . . . That means a heap of freezing days and snowfalls ahead of us this winter. . . . And corn shucks . . . they're thicker than I've ever seen them. . . ." He tossed the breast bone over his shoulder. "And that tells me we're fixing to have a hard winter. . . . Those signs don't never fail."

Talatu listened carefully and was surprised to find Shinn admitting that he was a conjurer. He could foretell the shape of weather for the days ahead from breastbones and shucks. Cherokee conjurers could not do that. Sometimes they could see what would happen to a person in the future by looking into their crystals, which were scales taken from the magic snake, the Uktena. Or the conjurers held beads in their hands and watched their movements to predict an epidemic of disease. But none had Shinn's power.

The sky darkened, and snow fell again, thick flakes that hissed and sputtered on the hot ashes.

"I ain't got a chance to finish the cabin," the white man went on. "There's a heap too much work still to be done." He shook his head sadly. "I never figured I'd be so slow a-raising a cabin."

Talatu looked up from his trencher at the log structure. Only a few rows of shingles covered the roof at one end, the walls were only partially chinked with mud, there was no chimney, and a doorway was still missing. He would never understand the ways of unegas. Cherokee would make an entrance as the walls were built. A chimney also, if it was wanted. Many elder Cherokee, like Old Coat, believed a hearth in the center of a house floor and a smokehole in the roof above warmed a house better than the white man's small fireplace and outside chimney.

"I reckon today I'd better make us a half-face shelter right here between those rocks," Shinn said. "With a fire in front of us and rocks behind and around us and a roof over our heads, we'll be snug as June bugs."

Shinn secured roof poles on the boulder tops. On these poles he placed layers of long canes sloping downward between the rocks, and then the shingles intended for the cabin over the cane. Talatu brought rocks and tree limbs to hold the shingles in place. Both of them gathered moss and leaves, which the snow had not yet touched to spread over the floor. The unega dumped his bedding on one side against the rock wall while Talatu spread his carefully on the other. His few possessions he placed on a little shelf jutting from the boulder beside his blanket.

Snow continued to fall. Shinn hitched up Shucky and snaked from the woods logs that had been felled and trimmed some time ago. These were for firewood. The Cricket sat in the open front of the shelter before the fire with his arms around his knees. His thoughts were at Chota, where Old Coat and his grandmother would be in their dirt-covered winter house. In this asi they would sit, dry and hot, eating chestnuts and telling stories. With all his heart he wished he was there with them.

As the days passed, Shinn's prophecy about the weather proved right. The snow now lay knee deep and crusted over with ice. And it was cold. The Cricket had never felt such cold. Wrapped in his blanket and sitting in the shelter before the fire, he still could not keep warm.

It was the morning when the snow stopped that Talatu's insides began to ache. By afternoon fire blazed in his belly, and searing flames shot through his chest. Had Shinn begun to work magic on him? Had the unega caused the food in his stomach to sprout? If so, he would slowly waste away and die. He was frightened.

Shinn paid him little mind when he quit work for the day. He staggered wet and weary to the fire, dried himself, ate, and fell into bed. Talatu slept little. All night the wind moaned through the trees. Once sleet came rattling down on the roof, shaking the shelter so hard that the boy feared it would not stand.

Dawn came, and Talatu rose, weak and dizzy. Shinn had sent the fire in his stomach up into his head and throat. He scooped up snow and pressed handfuls to his face. He crunched icicles and let the icy particles trickle slowly down his throat. When

Shinn stirred, the boy returned to his bed, feeling little better. Perhaps, he thought, the unega was shooting invisible bullets into him. It was one way a conjurer killed. But was Shinn's power strong enough to do that? He did not know.

Shinn stood and stretched and groaned. "Stiff as a board this morning," he remarked. While he ate, he glanced several times in the boy's direction. At last he came and squatted beside the Cricket.

"You look a mite feverish," he said. "And kinda peaked too." He reached out a hand and placed it on the boy's forehead.

"No!" screamed Talatu. He knocked the hand away. "Leave!" He pulled the blanket over his head.

"No need to be touchy," Shinn said briefly. "I had it in mind you might be sick." He stirred about for a while and then went out to cut firewood.

Once in the morning he came to the shelter and whispered, "Talatu . . . Cricket." The boy did not answer and kept his head covered. The unega went back to work.

Talatu slept fitfully and woke feeling full of pain. His skin was sore and tight, his flesh ached. He ran his hand over his cheek, and it felt rough. What was happening to him? He sat up and took his mirror from the rock shelf and stared at himself. Dark spots covered his forehead and cheeks. What had Shinn done to him?

Now his face was a mass of spots and his chest too. His throat was so dry that he could hardly swallow.

71

His heart leaped wildly against his ribs, and his head ached and burned. What was happening to him?

He had seen this before. In a flash of terror he saw his lips in the mirror move and form the awful word—smallpox! Shinn had not made food sprout in his belly or shot invisible bullets into him. He had done something much worse. He had sent smallpox into Talatu's body to kill him.

Cherokee conjurers feared smallpox above all sicknesses. Their powers and prayers and rituals were useless against it. There was nothing they could do to help those suffering or even to protect themselves. Shinn's evil power had succeeded. The boy knew he was doomed.

"I will never get to see Running Water Town and my young uncles," he thought in despair. "I will never get to take the warpath with Dragging Canoe."

Life among his kin and his friends had been sweet as a taste of the unega's sugar loaf. And now—now it was ending all too soon. He would never become a great warrior and leader like Old Coat. He would never be able to help the Cherokee Nation become strong and noble once again by driving the whites away. He would never—

Suddenly he laid the mirror aside. He had thought of something.

"I die—Shinn die," he told himself. "His death for my death. It is the way of Cherokee."

The rifle lay on the dry moss between their beds. He pulled it to him and made certain it was loaded.

Painfully he got to his feet and staggered from the shelter and fell to his knees. He was weaker than he had thought.

Crawling to the nearest boulder, he pulled himself up and braced his back against it to steady himself. He raised the rifle, aiming it toward Shinn, chopping wood with his back turned. The gun was heavy, and it took all Talatu's strength to hold the sights on the unega. He cocked the piece, ready to fire.

"Shinn!" he croaked. His throat was so dry that he could hardly speak. But he wanted the man to turn and see him and be frightened, as he himself had been frightened these past few days.

"Shinn!" he called again, and this time the white skin looked around. He dropped the ax and wiped the ice from the beard around his mouth. "Put down that rifle gun, Cricket," he said. He began to step slowly toward the boy.

Was that fear in those silver eyes? Talatu could not tell. It took all his willpower to hold the gun. One moment the rifle pointed at Shinn's breast, but before he could pull the trigger, the weapon wobbled almost out of his shaking hands.

He managed to bring it back and fought to hold it steady. But he was dizzy, and his knees were giving way, and he was sliding slowly down the side of the boulder. With one last great surge of strength he pointed the gun toward the unega and jerked at the trigger.

The gun roared.

Chapter 10

TALATU stood in a dazzling light before a council of white people. They were discussing whether he should be killed or allowed to live.

Mrs. Tilson was the leader. At last she spoke. "It is time to vote."

Shinn said, "Kill him."

The two men, Kirk and Tilson, shouted, "Kill! Kill!"

Mrs. Tilson smiled and began to chant, over and over, "Savage! Savage! Kill him!"

The boy and girl chanted with her and shook their tomahawks at the prisoner. "No! No!" screamed Talatu. He turned and ran. The whites came chasing behind him. On and on he sped, his feet pounding. But there was an army of unegas before him.

"Catch him!" they cried.

Talatu swerved and ran in another direction. White men and women popped out from behind trees and rocks in his path. He dodged this way and that, but it was no use; he was surrounded.

"Kill him!" the white people shouted and came

swarming from all directions and leaped on him, pressing him to the ground.

"No! Not kill me!" Talatu screamed.

Talatu screamed and screamed and finally quieted when he realized he was awake and the dream had passed. His throat was raw and his body limp with weariness and hurt. And his eyes—something was wrong with his eyes. He brushed his fingertips across them and found that his lids were swollen and sealed with oozing sores.

His thoughts came together, and he remembered that he lay in Shinn's shelter ill with the smallpox—and that he had shot Shinn.

Had he missed, he wondered? He listened, but the white man was not stirring about the camp.

"I killed him," he told himself. "I have revenge and—" Darkness rolled over him, and he slept again.

After that, he drifted in and out of sleep and fever dreams and wakefulness as if he were not an earth person but a ghost from the Darkening Land. Sometimes Shinn was there and sometimes he was missing, and Talatu could not tell whether the unega was alive only in his dreams or if he really existed.

Once he saw Shinn huddled around the fire talking to raccoons and opossums and one scrawny bobcat. Again the man was feeding him hot broth or rubbing salve on his chest. But he was not sure whether any of these things happened in truth.

He lay in a daze, floating like the Great Vulture

across the sky and seeing everything from far away. Then it seemed he was awake and staring at the fire in his grandmother's asi at Chota. But he heard his young uncles singing, and he knew he was with them in a dugout, going off to war. Once, he was certain his friend Swallow was at his side, washing his body and laughing at him for having a white man's sickness.

It was not his friend but his mother. She stood looking at him, wearing a turkey-red calico dress and the whitest of moccasins. Her hair was braided and coiled on top of her head and decorated with bright ribbons. She came through the mist and knelt beside him, combing his hair, untangling the knots in the gentle way she always did, and whispering, over and over, "*Hilunnu*. Go to sleep, little Cricket." He wanted to tell her it was not his fault he was weak and helpless, that Shinn had forced the evil into his body. With great effort he fought his way out of the hazy disorder of his dreams and opened his eyes.

For a moment he knew he was still dreaming. Shinn knelt beside his bed, running the bone comb through his hair, his roughened hands sure and gentle.

"Cricket!" the man exclaimed. "I figured you was better."

Shinn sounded both relieved and pleased that he was getting well, Talatu noted with surprise. Why was this since by his witchcraft Shinn had shot the smallpox into the Cricket's body? And had Shinn cared for him through his long spell of fever and pain? Why? Was the white man not a conjurer? Or had the strength of Old Coat's talisman kept the boy alive? Talatu did not know.

Then it occurred to him that the gods were protecting him. All his prayers to Thunder and the Provider and the Long Man had caught their attention, and they had aided him. It was the gods who had made him miss when he shot at Shinn so that the white man could live and save his life.

And he was alive!

"It is the way the gods want it," he assured himself. He would send them special prayers for listening to his pleas.

Talatu sat up. It took all his strength, and the shelter spun in dizzy circles around him. He waited until his head cleared. It would be a long time before he was strong enough to hunt again.

"I asked them folks here to help me with the cabin," the man remarked. "But I never figured they'd bring the smallpox with them—that boy of Kirk's died from it."

Then Shinn had not used his magic power to give him the smallpox? Could that be the truth?

"And looky yonder," Shinn said, pointing. "All that work wasted."

Two pine trees had fallen across the cabin and crushed the roof and scattered the log walls. Trees lay on the ground in a jumble. Some had split in two and fallen; others had broken and left only a shattered part of their trunks standing.

"Trees down everywhere," Shinn told him. "Got top-heavy from too much ice and snow. And it was so almighty cold that the sap in that maple yonder froze and it busted wide open. Animals froze to death all out through the woods. You going to have trouble finding something alive to shoot when you get back to hunting again."

He laughed. "I reckon you figured my skin was worth something in trade. When you first took sick, you got flighty-headed and tried to shoot me." He laughed again. "You missed, you were so shaky. But it's mighty hard to find anything to miss these days."

No game! That would be as bad for Talatu as it was for those at Chota. His people depended on deer-skins for trading. And he needed skins for a rifle. He accepted a mug of broth from Shinn. It was good.

"You hunt deer—for this," the Cricket asked, holding out his mug for more.

The man shook his head. "No sirree, no need to," he explained. "I took my ax out in the woods and chopped a haunch off a deer I found froze to death. Some folks don't hold with eating meat less'n it's fresh killed. Say it's tainted. Not me."

Talatu did not quite understand what Shinn meant. He swallowed more broth. How good it tasted! But the weight of the mug made his hands shake. He set it down slowly and lay back on his blanket.

"Some of them nights were so cold," Shinn continued, "that I had to sleep with one hand and put wood on the fire with the other."

He burst out laughing, then sobered and added, "But for a fact now, raccoons and 'possums came and sat around my fire with me many a cold night, and once a mangy old bobcat joined us and purred as he warmed hisself. Takes powerful cold weather to make varmints do such as that."

He poked at the fire now. "You was sick a long time," he added. "The smallpox was bad, but the side pleurisy that came after it was worse. I made sure when you got the galloping consumption, that was the last of your sickness. No sir, seemed like the colder it got, the sicker you got. I nearabout ran out of things to doctor you with."

He laughed. "I kept the bear grease heating on the fire so I could rub it on your chest, but even boiling there was a skim of ice on top of it. I had to bust the ice to use it."

"Sick—long time?" asked the Cricket weakly.

"Sure enough," Shinn replied. "All them fevers made you miss the coldest weather we ever had in these parts. I reckon that was lucky. But it's most over now, and looks like you're fixing to take a turn for the better too."

He touched Talatu's cheek. "You got some scars.

I've seen worse. You're young. They'll get where you can't see them in a few years."

He picked up the mug and, lifting Talatu's head gently, helped him drink a little more of the broth. The boy appreciated it. Without thinking, he thanked the man in Cherokee, "Wadan, Shinn—wadan."

"No call to thank me," Shinn said and grinned. "We got to get you back on your feet soon. And put some meat on your bones. You look like you was made out of ribs."

It took Talatu a moment to realize that the white skin had understood his Cherokee. Strange, he thought. If Shinn knew the language of Talatu's people, why did he not speak it to him? He shut his eyes. He was too tired to think about it now.

Chapter 11

THE VOICES of geese dropped from the sky over the clearing. Talatu glanced up. A large flock was flying north in arrowpoint formation behind a noisy leader. Long after they passed from sight, he could still hear those piercing calls.

"Dagulku," he murmured and smiled, remembering the story Old Coat often told as he filled his pipe bowl. "The goose that stole tobacco long ago from the Cherokee and carried it far to the south."

Suddenly misery and loneliness and homesickness gripped him so that his heart twisted in his chest and tears filled his eyes. He was desperate for a sight of Chota, longed to hear his great-uncle's stories again and to feel his grandmother's warm arms securely about him. It seemed years since he had left his mother. How he missed her! So much pain, so much sorrow had befallen him in those months. And it had all come to nothing! His path here at Watauga had been weary and baffling. He did not understand why Old Coat had sent him anyway. He did not know how much longer he could stand to live away from his own land and his own people.

"It is not right," he told himself, "that a Cherokee be kept so long from his homeland."

From the rock shelf beside his bed, he picked up Old Coat's talisman and held it tightly. It leaped in his hands like a wild thing. Its strength flowed into his arms and body and burned away the ache of homesickness and left him comforted with hope.

Outside, woodpeckers drummed on trees and frogs sang and shiny new leaves fluttered in the warm sunlight. It was spring. By the end of summer he would be heading back to Chota. He could wait that long. He would not enjoy the passing days, but he would endure.

"I have not been cut away from my people," he asserted. "I am not lost by living among the unegas. I am Talatu of the Wolf Clan and one of the Principal People always."

At last he decided to take the rifle and walk out through the woods. Lately, his luck had been bad, for the terrible winter had made game scarce. Kanati, who kept the earth's animals in a cave, had not allowed any of them to come out to restock the forests. All of Talatu's prayers to the ancient keeper of game had gone unnoticed. Today he would not bother with any hunting rituals.

Leaving the clearing, he crossed the creek and made his way to the edge of the woods where Shinn worked. The man was busy girdling the trees with his ax, chopping circlets of bark from the trunks to kill them. Those that had fallen during the icy weather he was burning. Flames curled through the piles of brush, hurling smoke and sparks high in the air.

It was the same way his people prepared a new field, and Talatu had no doubt that the Watauga white skins had learned the methods from the Cherokee. Later, Shinn would plant corn between the standing trunks. Talatu hoped the crop would be plentiful, for there had been no cornmeal for them to eat for a long time. And he liked cornmeal dumplings. When he ate them, the taste was the same as the taste of Neeroree's dumplings. It was like being at home once more.

Talatu pushed on, detouring around a tangle of fallen trees and picking his way carefully down a hillside among anemone and trilliums, their flowers bright among the rock slides. He passed along a canebrake, flattened by the winter's ice, and crossed a meadow white with strawberry flowers. The meadow was marked here and there by the skeletons of raccoons and the decomposed body of a deer.

The day was warm and the air fresh and sweet. The trees shimmered in their new leaves. It was good to be out in the woods even if this was the land of the unegas. And it was good that spring had returned to the earth as it had in times past. Somehow he had expected the ferocity of the winter, along with his own illness, to hold spring back. Yet it was here for him to enjoy as much as he always had in his homeland.

He stopped at the edge of an old field grown up in

coarse grass and pines and sumac saplings. Off to one side in the tall trees a flock of vultures whispered and hissed and spread their wings in lazy fashion. He knew they had feasted well this spring on the carrion.

He moved away from the roost with its stench of rotten flesh and walked along the field's edge. Once he caught a glimpse of a band of wolves running in and out among the trees. They were gaunt and bony, for the winter's dead did not appeal to them. Only the old ones whose teeth were worn and useless subsisted on putrid meat, he knew. The others took it only if they must.

"Ah, brothers," he called after them, "hungry times ahead for you and me. Fresh-killed game will be scarce."

He continued along the outskirts of the field, hoping for a shot at a groundhog, but he was disappointed. Close by, a dog barked, and then there was shouting. He turned back. He was uneasy about meeting any of the Watauga whites. They might harm him, alone and far from Shinn's clearing, or take the rifle from him.

At a spring he came on a fire, the ashes still warm. It was so near the settlement, he wondered why anyone would camp here. At the edge of the fire lay a stone streaked with red. He sucked in his breath and picked it up with shaking fingers.

War paint!

Red powder had been mixed with water on the stone. He rubbed his finger in the mixture, and his

84

finger came away smeared with the paint. Cherokee painted themselves before going into battle. A war party was nearby—there was no doubt about it.

His heart almost stopped. Dragging Canoe! His young uncles! Friends from home, here at Watauga. He glanced about excitedly. If he could find the warriors, he would go with them, take Shinn's rifle and leave and never be sad about departing.

In the mud around the spring were many prints of Cherokee moccasins. There was also the mark of a white man's boot. That surprised him. He did not know that the Canoe had friends in Watauga.

A little path led off into the trees. He followed it at a trot, not sure the warriors had gone this way, for leaves covered the path. But farther along, at a stream, the prints were plain. Now two white men led the war party. He was truly puzzled. What kind of war party was this, led by white men? What kind of Cherokee warriors would let white men tell them how to wage war?

Leaping to the far bank, he ran as fast as he could in and out among the trees. At last the path veered out of the woods and into an old cornfield. He looked about among the weathered stalks and cockleburs but saw no sign of anyone. Had he lost the war party?

Suddenly from ahead came shrill cries.

"Whoo whoop! whoooo whoop!"

It was the Cherokee war shout. There was rifle fire, and a man yelled, "Run, Martha, for God's sake, run!"

Talatu sprinted across the field and into the thick undergrowth at the far side. He floundered about, pushing blindly through, catching the rifle in vines. He tripped and fell and had to fight to free himself. He began to crawl, twisting and struggling. Then he was out and in a clearing.

He stood up, looking about. There was a cowshed near him and, some distance beyond, a cabin. The roof was on fire, and smoke poured from the open doorway. On the ground lay two unegas. Three naked painted warriors came out of the cabin door. Two of them stopped and scalped the dead whites, the other ripped open the bedding he carried. He began to run, dragging the featherbed and scattering the feathers.

Talatu leaped forward, screaming desperately, but the warriors did not look around. They had not heard him. He rounded the shed and found the bodies of a boy and a cow. Ahead he saw the Indians disappear into the woods. He kept running, too breathless to shout any longer.

At last he halted and searched among the trees for one of his people. There was no one in sight. He was too late. Not a warrior had seen or heard him. Now he would never find them, for the war party would be traveling fast, raiding other cabins and heading back toward the Canoe's towns.

Still, he thought, one warrior might be lingering close enough to hear. He took a deep breath and shouted, "Tsiyugunsini! Tsiyugunsini!"

Dragging Canoe's name would bring any Cherokee who was near. He waited, listening. It was quiet. The cabin burned with crackling and popping noises behind him. It seemed strange to Cricket to be waiting here in the white man's land to be rescued by an unexpected Cherokee war party. It was another of those fever dreams he had had while he was ill.

He heard someone scuffling through the leaves toward him, and he knew it was no warrior. He crouched behind a bush. Back among the tree shadows, he saw not one but two figures approaching. They were unegas, and they were coming from the direction in which the war party had disappeared. Were they the two white men who had been with the warriors?

One he had never seen before, but the other was the opossum-faced man he had seen at the store. They might have been with the war party, but Felton Tyce could not be anything but an enemy. He was surely not the kind of white man the Canoe would befriend. Talatu remembered the hot shame of that day when Tyce had cut the thong that held his breechclout.

Had they seen him? He did not know, but he crawled away as fast as he could, hiding behind laurel bushes. At last he stood and ran. He glanced over his shoulder, but the two whites were not in sight.

As he recrossed the cornfield, five men came riding out of the woods. He walked slowly on, and when the men came up to him, they reined to a halt.

"It's Shinn's savage," one said.

"We heard shooting," another added. "You know about it?"

Talatu understood but did not answer. What was there to say? He was frightened.

"He ain't likely to understand you," the first man remarked. "Injuns ain't got but the least little bit of sense."

"Yonder comes somebody," one said.

Talatu turned and saw Tyce and his companion running through the corn stalks. They had seen him then, in spite of his efforts to hide, and had followed. He was caught! Suddenly he remembered how he had told Old Coat that fear of whites had no place in his thoughts. That was the talk of a child, not of a warrior, for his spirit did not stand as tall now as those brave words. At this moment all his thoughts were fear.

"Him—him's the one I seen," Tyce panted as he came up. "Guiding a war party—killed the Greens—"

"Killed the Greens!" one of the riders exclaimed in a horrified voice. "All of 'em?"

"Me and Crawford been hunting—heard war whoops." Tyce talked on. "Got there too late to help—seen him there—Shinn's Injun—we been chasing him."

"My woman's alone in the cabin! She might not have heard them shots," cried another of the riders. "Lots of folks might not. We got to go tell." He wheeled his horse around and rushed off.

"Don't let the savage get away," a third yelled over his shoulder. And then they were gone in a crashing gallop, and Talatu was alone. Over him loomed the hateful hating faces of the two white men.

In Tyce's eyes he saw a lifetime of meanness. A glance at the other man brought him no comfort either. They would torture him—he knew they would—and he would not be able to stand the pain. He would disgrace his young uncles.

Tyce snatched the rifle from the Cricket and used it to prod him across the field.

Chapter 12

"CRAWFORD, reckon his scalp's worth anything?" Tyce asked his companion as they neared the far side of the field.

"Not to you, once Shinn found out you scalped him," Crawford replied.

Tyce turned on his companion with a snarl. "You reckon Shinn scares me?"

"Maybe not, but I seen him in a rage that wasn't good for his peace-loving Quaker soul," Crawford answered. "He scared me."

"Shinn ain't a Quaker anymore," Tyce told him, and he laughed. "He's a Tory now, for we're going to pin this raid to his shirttails afore anybody tries to pin it to us. Lucky this boy came along when he did. We can fix Shinn good, spread the word that him and his savage been spying for Dragging Canoe. Time we're through, the Committee of Safety will run him out of Watauga, for sure."

Crawford laughed. "Tyce, you're a wonder," he said. "But you ain't said what you aim to do with the little savage."

"Well, Old Man Knowles said, don't let him get

away," Tyce pointed out, "but he never said we had to stay and guard him. We'll tie him up good and proper. We got work to do. I know a couple of ears just waiting for some tattle about Shinn."

They pushed through the brush into the Greens' clearing and began to cross.

Tyce went on. "I reckon folks'll soon be coming to bury the Greens," he said. "Can't leave them out for the varmints. We'll let the burying party take care of him."

Crawford nodded as the two of them halted before the shed. Flies swarmed around the faces of the boy and the cow. Talatu looked away. He wondered if he would end up beside them.

Tyce went into the shed. "Looky here," he exclaimed from inside. "Pine tar. Crawford, go get that featherbed over yonder."

He came back carrying some thongs and a wooden piggin. Using the thongs he bound Talatu's hands and feet and tied him to a fence post. Then he pulled the paddle from the bucket and began to smear the sticky, runny sap over Talatu's naked chest and legs. He smudged streaks of tar down the boy's arms and finally over his head.

He dropped the paddle back into the piggin and remarked, "Injuns like wearing feathers, Crawford, we'll let him wear aplenty."

The two white men pulled handfuls of feathers from the torn ticking and flung them over the Cricket until he looked like a half-feathered duck. Talatu thought that if this was the white man's torture, it was foolish. Still, he was glad none of the war party was around to see him, or any of his kin. He was shamed.

"Now they will kill me," he told himself. He braced so as not to cry out or show fear. Would Shinn take his bones back to Chota for burial? It would be terrible to be left here in unfamiliar earth.

Tyce stepped away and admired their handiwork. "Mighty handsome," he grinned. "Let's go."

They picked up their weapons and walked off into the woods. In shock and relief, Talatu watched them go.

It was quiet after the two men left. Talatu slumped against the post. The pine tar stung and burned where his skin was still marked and sensitive from the pox. He had thought the white men would surely kill him, and he was proud that he had not flinched or let fear make him tremble. He had been a real warrior.

But soon the others would come to bury the dead white man and woman and their child. These others would kill him, he knew. They would not wait to find out who he was or why he was there.

Oh, if he had only been a little bit quicker! If he had only arrived here a breath or so earlier, he could have caught the war party and left with them. If only . . .

He saw a shadow passing and glanced up to find a vulture swooping overhead. If the white people did not arrive soon to bury their dead, they would be too late. Another black tilting shape floated over and then another.

"Suli, you have come for a feast," he called softly. "But you will not feast on me."

Crawford had taken the Cricket's knife, but Shinn's rifle and pouch and shot bag lay nearby. He could free himself from these thongs and take his gear and leave before anyone else got there. He would beg Shinn to clean this disgraceful coat of feathers from him and take him home, for he had had more than enough of Watauga and the strange ways of white skins.

Now he set to work, rubbing the thongs about his arms up and down against the post behind him. Perhaps he could break or wear them through. All he managed to do was scrape the skin from his wrists.

He would loosen the post and pull it from the ground. It would not be deeply set. He strained forward then slammed himself back, again and again, until he was too weary to go on. But still the post stood firm.

He should have dug around the post with his feet before he tried so hard, he thought.

Now he kicked and gouged at the earth around the log, but he was weak and sore from his other efforts, and it was no use. Suli would, after all, gorge on Cherokee flesh this day.

He waited in the growing heat, and the tar was sticky and uncomfortable and itched. He did not understand the unegas. Why had they done this stupid thing to him? He vaguely understood that they had decided that it was the Cricket who had led the war party here to attack the cabin.

Why had they not killed him outright? Why had they left him for the others to find?

He saw the group of whites long before they saw him. They came out of the woods and stood quietly at its edge, looking warily around. Two women rode horseback, but the men were on foot and carried rifles. Talatu tensed himself and prayed to the Ancient Red to make his spirit strong so that he could face his enemies bravely and properly, as one of the Real People should.

Slowly the men circled the clearing and the smoking ruins of the cabin. The Cricket could have told them that the warriors had long gone and were halfway back to Chota by this time. But the white men went watchfully and stealthily, as though the Indians might be lurking under stones.

One of them came toward the shed. He spied Talatu and let out a whoop. "Here's the one they was talking about!" he yelled. "Here's Shinn's little savage!"

A couple of the others ran forward. One of them raised a gun and aimed it right at him, not a dozen yards away. Talatu stood very still, holding his breath, staring along the rifle barrel to the man's eye behind the back sight.

A second man struck down the weapon quickly.

"No call to waste lead," he spoke cruelly. "We can take him apart with a couple of knives."

The man who had first discovered the Cricket unslung his tomahawk. "I can start with taking off his scalp," he said. "Slow and easy, so it'll be in one good piece." The man stepped closer.

Such hatred and loathing burned from the eyes of all the white men that Talatu could almost feel it, like the burn of the tar on his still-tender skin. He stood as straight as he could and stared ahead and tried to look as though he thought less of these men than of the flies that flew around the clearing.

The tomahawk came nearer. The sun flashed on the sharp-honed edge of the metal blade. He felt his life going from him, and his breathing seemed to stop. The Darkening Land opened, and the ghosts of his ancestors awaited his coming.

"Great day in the morning!" a voice shouted. "What you up to, Wells? Ain't you got a pinch of sense? Let the boy alone."

It was Kirk. Out of the corner of his eye Talatu saw Shinn's friend hurrying up.

"He done it!" cried Wells. "He led the party here to do the killing! Tyce saw him." But he lowered his arm.

"Tyce!" Kirk's voice was scornful. "Tyce can see two deer, and it looks like a herd of buffalo to him. He can't tell the truth even when he knows what it is, and he does a heap of lying."

Kirk moved up beside the boy. "You know Shinn's

savage just ain't any little Injun," he went on. "He's got a heap of kin that has a mighty lot of say-so with the Cherokees. They done let Shinn have him to take care of, and they ain't going to be pleased if something happens to him. There'll be a heap of burying around here."

The man who had threatened to shoot the Cricket looked up. "That's right," he muttered. "And I done see that happen once too often."

The man with the tomahawk cursed. "Let 'em try it," he cried.

"Shut up, Wells," said Kirk. "You ain't got no cabin nor no young 'uns."

He untied Talatu and spoke to the others. "I'll take him on back to Shinn's. If Tyce got any way to prove what he said, he can talk to Shinn and the Committee of Safety about it."

Shinn was standing beside the ruined cabin sharpening his ax blade with a stone when Kirk and Talatu arrived at the clearing. He dropped the ax and whetstone when he saw them crossing toward him.

"Trouble?" he asked Kirk, and a worried frown creased his forehead.

"Tyce," answered Kirk shortly. "Chickamaugas killed the Greens, all of them, and Tyce and Crawford claim to have seen your little Injun leading the way."

The Cricket knew the silly way the white men spoke of the Canoe's followers as "Chickamauga" because they once lived along the creek of that name.

But they were Cherokee still, the bravest and best of the warriors, still willing to fight and kill their enemies.

He stood by the two men, silent and still, with the itching feathers and tar beginning to draw and pull at his chest and back and arms. He gave no sign. No one would ever see him revealing that this foolish treatment had affected him at all.

Shinn bent over him and put a hand under his chin and tilted his face up so that Talatu was looking into the water-pale eyes. "You didn't do no such thing, did you, Cricket?" the man asked slowly.

With all his heart Talatu wanted to cry out, "Yes, yes! I helped my people kill the fool white man and his wife. I showed them the way! I would do it again." But he could not lie to Shinn somehow. And somehow Shinn would know he was lying.

Slowly the boy shook his head. "No. Found fire— found paint—many moccasin prints." He paused and looked steadily at Shinn. "White men shoeprint there—white men, two white men."

Shinn and Kirk exchanged startled looks. "White men?" Shinn repeated. His grasp tightened. "You sure?"

Talatu made no response, nor did he glance away. Shinn dropped his hand.

Kirk said softly, "The Greens had powder stored at their place. For the militia. So if 'twas white men led the Injuns, it was some from hereabouts that knew where the powder was hid."

"Don't say such!" Shinn exclaimed. "Tories! Neighbors! I thought all the Tories had been run out."

"Neighbors can be Tories and never let on," Kirk said reasonably.

Shinn had told the Cricket that Tories were those white men who were loyal to the king across the water. Talatu was not very interested in the white men's squabbles among themselves, except now he knew it must be these Tories who sometimes supplied Dragging Canoe and his warriors with arms and powder for raids. But then, why would Tories treat him so badly?

Shinn was still looking dismayed. Finally he said, "You reckon it could be Tyce and Crawford? They ain't never seemed like honest men to me."

"Tyce is a master hand at lying and stirring up trouble," Kirk answered. "Nobody ain't labeled him Tory yet, though. But you—" He paused and looked levelly at Shinn. "You don't never fight with the militia, and you got your little savage here with you. There's a heap of folks wouldn't mind calling you Tory. And Tyce will be out early and late to give you the name. Trouble's knocking at your door."

"And that's a fact," Shinn agreed. "I thank you for the warning and your friendship."

Kirk went his way.

Shinn put his hand on Talatu's shoulder. "Come on, we'll clean you up," was all he said.

He heated some bear grease and rubbed it over and

over the tarry places and then scoured it off with lye soap and sand. The scouring hurt worse than the pitch had done, but the feathers and a lot of the pine tar gradually came off.

"The rest'll come off in time," Shinn said finally. "But we ain't got much time left here. I got to think about getting you back to Chota sometime soon. I didn't bring you here to get you in trouble."

Back to Chota! Back to Chota! The words sang in the Cricket's head. Back to Chota! He was going home.

Chapter 13

THE SUMMER passed slowly for Talatu. It was difficult to wait here in the white man's land when he longed to be in his own country, among his own people. He asked Thunder to hurry the days so he could leave. But in his heart he knew it was useless to pray. Between dawn and sunset stretched a lifetime. He carried each day on his shoulders like a load of heavy stones.

He and Shinn hunted and fished. They chopped weeds from around the fast-growing corn. He would not be here to eat Shinn's corn. He would surely be in Running Water Town when the corn was harvested and would take part in the Green Corn Dance with his mother and young uncles. That was a happy thought, and he worked back and forth across the field, chopping the weeds fiercely, each stroke a dead Wataugan.

"Tomorrow, Shinn?" he asked. "Tomorrow we go?"

"Soon, Cricket, any day now," the unega replied.

At night they sat near the fire. Whippoorwills called to each other up and down the creek banks, and every now and then a toad's sad trill echoed over the water. The night sounds were the same along the Tennessee River, and closing his eyes, Talatu imagined he was back home.

Often Shinn talked. He told how to kill witches with a silver bullet. He said that Old Coat's gorget was believed by whites to be a thunderstone fallen from the sky. It was good luck to find one. He told about the time he had found a rock in which there was a tiny coiled snake.

One night they saw a bright star shoot across the sky. Shinn had told Talatu so much that the boy thought out of politeness he should tell Shinn something.

"Long time back," he began, "some Cherokee hunters found star creatures."

The stars had tiny heads, like turtle heads, sticking from their fat bodies. They were covered with downy feathers. They had no tongues and could not answer the questions the hunters asked them. The stars stayed with the hunters for a few days, then one night rose up into the sky and never returned.

He ended, "That is what the old men tell."

"My gravy," said Shinn politely. Talatu could tell he did not believe the story.

August thunderheads filled the sky and shook the clearing, and summer was passing. Talatu worried. Why had they not left for Chota?

Kirk visited them, bringing a sack of cornmeal. He and Shinn talked earnestly for a long time. After a while the Cricket crept close to listen. Shinn was speaking.

"I don't take to all this fighting and killing," he exclaimed. "I don't serve in the militia with the folks from Watauga, so folks around here think I'm a Tory. And if the British come over the mountains, they'll shoot me along with the rest of the Wataugan rebels."

Talatu had never understood why whites who spoke the same language and looked the same and had the same customs should kill one another and plunder one another's homes. What a foolish way to behave! Cherokee never fought against other Cherokee; never did one town fight another, or one whole settlement of towns wage warfare against another Cherokee settlement. They might disagree, but one side always withdrew from the argument before their differences led to bloodshed.

" 'Fight and kill with us, or you're our enemy,' folks around here tell me," said Shinn. "But I ain't fixing to kill anybody. I've seen a heap too many die for no good reason. So I volunteered to do scouting duty with Colonel Sevier some time ago. When he sends for me, I'll go, but I said I wouldn't kill anybody and I meant it!"

"I believe you," said Kirk with a nod as he left.

The boy sat in silence for a while. When you lived surrounded by white and Indian enemies, as the Cherokee had for so long, you killed or you got killed when the time arose. All Talatu's life he lived with this belief, so it was not a thing to worry over. A warrior tried to die a brave death. He tried to take his enemy with him to the Darkening Land. Your enemy, too, tried to die a brave death. It seemed right. He did not understand Shinn's feelings. Yet somehow—somehow they made Shinn seem a good man, a strong warrior.

At last he asked, "Man bring news? News I go home?"

Shinn shook his head. The Wataugans were expecting another Chickamauga raid, and all the paths were guarded, he said.

"We got to wait a bit," Shinn went on. "Folks around here don't take to us one little bit. They wouldn't like it if we set out for one of Dragging Canoe's towns. They'd figure we was taking information to the Canoe."

Talatu was disappointed. But what was there to do? He could see that Shinn was not happy either. Something was troubling him.

One bright autumn day Shinn said he would go and see how things were with the Wataugans. "I reckon things are clear by now," he said, "and me and you can head south to your home."

He paused. "If anybody comes—*anybody*—" he repeated with force, "let 'em be. Don't show yourself. Understand?"

The Cricket nodded. He did not want any white skins to see him either. He glanced up and saw that the man's misty pale eyes were not on him—they were seeing things elsewhere. Something was still troubling him, the boy thought.

The next day Shinn rode away on Shucky, and Talatu climbed to the top of the cliff with his blanket and a piece of smoked meat. The Day Dweller hardly seemed to move across the sky. And Talatu was lonely. Already he missed Shinn. Somehow he had come to like the white man. He had long since ceased to believe that Shinn was a conjurer or was trying to harm him. Shinn had made him well by careful nursing, he was sure. They had shared cold and hunger and worked hard together. And in a strange way his ugly thoughts about the unega had gone away.

Shinn was back in two days with bad news.

"South Carolina is in British hands," he explained. "And North Carolina will soon be, it's said. Major Ferguson has sent a message saying he's going to come over the mountains and hang all our chief men."

He smiled a little. "He'll march his army over the mountains, hang the leaders, and lay the country waste with fire and sword. That's how the words went, folks say. Kind of elegant talk for us woodsies."

Talatu waited. Shinn had more to say. "You and me got to leave, and mighty soon. Two days from now."

The Cricket's heart leaped. Shinn would find a way to take him back to Chota, perhaps even to Running Water Town.

"Remember I promised Colonel Sevier I'd be a scout?" the man asked. "Well, I'm going with the militia over the mountains to spy out the land and see what Ferguson is up to. And I'll have to take you too."

Over the mountains? Eastward, not south to Chota? Anger and disappointment almost choked Talatu. Shinn would never let him go home!

Chapter 14

THE RACKET echoed back among the trees to greet Shinn and Talatu long before they arrived at the militia's gathering place at Sycamore Shoals.

The woods began to thin, and now the boy could see the white people who were creating the commotion. Children ran screaming through the crowd, dogs barking at their heels. To one side a herd of cattle bawled and shifted about. New arrivals came riding up in a steady stream, calling out loudly to friends.

The Cricket drew in his breath. Unegas everywhere—they swarmed among the sycamore and pawpaw trees along the riverbank, filled the fields in overwhelming numbers as far as he could see. It was a terrifying sight, all those soldiers and guns. Who would have thought there could be so many white skins assembled in one place? He hoped Shinn did not expect him to go among them. His courage was not that strong.

Shinn handed the horse's lead line to the boy and gave him the rifle. "Wait here while I have a word with Colonel Sevier," he told him.

Talatu glanced about uneasily. He saw Kirk and Tilson with their families. Shinn stopped to talk to them a moment and moved on to speak to a man better dressed than most of those around him. Was that one of their leaders, the boy wondered? And then he caught a glimpse of Tyce, tying his horse's reins to a sapling and joining Crawford and another man at a campfire.

Were Tyce and Crawford going to fight with these Americans? Then the two never could be Tories, as Shinn had speculated. He did not want to be seen by them, no matter which side they chose to fight on.

He led Shucky back into the woods where they would be better hidden. A man passed nearby, singing, and Talatu thought it was Shinn, but the singer went on. He waited, shifting about and fingering Old Coat's charm, which hung about his neck under his shirt. Would its power be with him a little longer, so that he might yet live to reach home?

During the summer Talatu had come to believe that Shinn was a good man. Now he could see that his heart was rotten and black. All the promises the man had made about getting him back to Chota had been lies along a crooked path. The Cricket was furious with himself for believing what he had been told. He should have known better. White men had always lied to his people, cheated them out of their lands, killed them after swearing to spare them.

Shinn returned and took the horse's line. "We'll go on ahead, to make sure there ain't no British hiding along the path," he said. "You keep a sharp eye out, Cricket. You're as good a scout as any man, I reckon."

Talatu nodded, moving off behind the man with the gun cradled in his arms. This would be better than marching surrounded by a unega army, where he would not be able to take an easy breath or be free from fear.

They followed the streams, winding their way eastward toward tall, hazy mountains. Then they were climbing through thick-bodied trees and yellowing feathery ferns, up and up. It was cold and damp. Once they came on a beech wood, golden with sunlight, and back among the silvery boles, they glimpsed turkeys and deer feeding. They flushed a brood of young grouse from among the laurel shrubs.

Over the mountains and down a gorge with cracked bluffs looming overhead and tree falls everywhere. There were many places for an ambush, and Shinn moved carefully, sometimes scouting alongside the path and up the slopes while Talatu waited on the trail.

On the second day they once again began to climb. By afternoon they were walking in ankle-deep snow.

"One thing about snow," remarked Shinn. "It may be cold, but it sure makes tracking easy. Ain't been a man this way lately, or we'd see his traces. There's no way a body can hide his tracks in snow good enough to fool anybody."

At last they left the dark wooded slopes and

stepped out onto a wide meadow. The dazzling snow struck Talatu's eyes almost as if a fist had rammed into them. He flinched and turned quickly away, following Shinn to the mountain's rocky edge.

Below, the snow-free ridges and mountain peaks were piled in great blue-green lumps and red-brown angles westward toward Watauga. It was breathtaking, awesome! Talatu had never been so high or had such a view of the far-reaching, world-old mountains, given to his people by the gods after the Great Vulture had shaped them with the sweet and gentle touch of its outspread wings.

Old Coat had always said the mountains were like wrinkled grandfathers that had protected the Cherokee since time out of mind. But how much longer, Talatu wondered, could the grandfather mountains keep the white men away? The trail that he and Shinn followed had already been taken over and widened and changed by the whites, as if it belonged to them. Tomorrow it would be a valley the Cherokee lost, then the ridges, until all this beautiful land would be taken by the greedy unegas.

Anger surged through him. These were his very own mountains. The bones of his ancestors were buried here; the rivers and ranges had Cherokee names—he did not want the white skins to take them! He was willing to give his life to keep them for his people. Oh, if he could only fight at the side of his young uncles and Dragging Canoe.

A year, more than a year, and still he waited. Now

he was old enough surely, strong enough surely, to fight with them. How did he come to be here with these men who went to fight without knowing what land this was or how it came to be?

"Yonder's where the army is," Shinn said, pointing out the smoke rising from the campfires in the dark woods of the valley. "They're making good time. Anxious to get at Ferguson, I reckon. I don't want to get too far ahead of them. We won't leave so early in the morning."

The man turned back to the packhorse tied to a fire cherry tree. "Now let's eat right through this turkey I was lucky enough to shoot today." He grinned at the boy and added, "We'll fry up the gobble and eat it first off, and then chomp our way right on through to the tail feathers."

Talatu did not smile back.

The next morning Shinn kept them in camp while he patched his moccasins. Then they proceeded down the eastern slope of the mountain. By mid-afternoon they were walking through a crooked, twisting valley. Shinn was debating whether to stop for the night when they heard horses galloping along the path toward them.

"Who in creation?" Shinn muttered. He pulled the boy and horse off the trail.

Three riders came racing past them—Tyce and Crawford and one other. They were whipping their horses and riding hard, glancing back over their shoulders every so often. The man and the boy in the undergrowth went unnoticed.

"I'd give a pretty to know what they're up to," Shinn mused. "Nothing good, that's for sure."

They walked on and stopped when the light began to leave the valley. Shinn had just taken their bundles from the packsaddle on Shucky when once again they heard hoofbeats.

"Now who?" muttered Shinn.

It was Kirk and Wells. Shinn yelled out to them. The two riders turned and came back.

Another of his enemies, thought Talatu. Wells was the one who had almost ended his life with a tomahawk at the Greens' clearing. Kirk had saved him, but the man was only Shinn's friend. Kirk had no more love for Indians than Wells.

"You fellers out riding for your health?" asked Shinn.

"You might say that," replied Kirk. "We aim to catch three deserters before they get to Ferguson and tell him about the over-mountain men coming after him."

"Deserters? Sure?" Shinn wanted to know.

"You know that wide meadow atop the mountain back yonder?" Wells asked. "We stopped there to have roll call and parade about and check our weapons. At roll call Tyce and Crawford and Chambers had skeedaddled pretty as you please with not a word to nobody."

"Sevier sent us to catch them," Kirk went on. "He and the other commanders don't like it a bit. They didn't want Ferguson to know how many men we got."

"We got to get on," Wells pointed out. "Run 'em down and shoot 'em. That's our orders."

"You ain't got a chance to catch them three," Shinn told him. "The way they shot past us, they've done reached the ocean by now."

"I sure wish we could get our hands on those three," exclaimed Wells. "I hate a Tory worse than the Devil."

Shinn looked at him levelly. "A man's got a right to believe in what he wants," he said finally. "Trouble with Tyce, he don't believe in nothing. He killed the Greens for silver, pure and simple. Not for England, nor for the king, just for himself. He has always struck me as a feller that would be on whatever side paid best. And I reckon Ferguson will reward him right well for information on the over-mountain army."

Wells groaned, and both riders dismounted.

"We'll just camp with you tonight," Kirk said. "Tomorrow you forget scouting and get to spying. That's what Nolichucky Jack Sevier said. He's going to take a safer trail north of this one. But we got to know where Ferguson is, else we ain't going to have no fight. And it'll be your lookout to find him."

Talatu stood to one side, trying to follow the talk. He understood enough to make him uneasy. It seemed to him that Tyce was always around to give him trouble. The man was sure to be somewhere ahead, waiting for him, and Talatu did not like it.

He was afraid of this man who hated Shinn and whose presence made Shinn look the way he never looked at any other time. He was afraid for himself, and strangely, sickeningly, he was afraid for Shinn.

Chapter 15

Two DAYS LATER, Talatu and the three men reached the settlement of Quaker Meadows.

"We'll wait here for our over-mountain men," Kirk said.

Talatu knew what the words "over-mountain men" meant—those whites who had come westward over the Cherokee mountains to settle on his people's land at Watauga and other places. Why had Old Coat and the other Principal Warriors of the Cherokee Nation let them stay when they first arrived? It was a question no one ever answered. The event had happened, and the Cherokee had accepted it for a while. But it had brought a troubled change in Cherokee life, and now Dragging Canoe wanted to undo the past and drive the white skins away and lead his people back to their old ways.

Shinn unbuckled the straps that held the pack-saddle on Shucky. He lifted it to the ground and said, "I reckon if you two are staying here, we part company then."

He began to unpack the canvas in which their possessions had traveled. To one side he placed the pack-saddle frame, and around it he put a skillet and a small iron pot, then a lead bar and bullet mold, a bag of powder and an extra blanket.

"Me and Cricket got to travel fast and light," Shinn said to Kirk. "Leave that packsaddle and truck at Colonel McDowell's place, and I'll pick it up coming back."

Joseph McDowell was a militia colonel, commander of American forces on the southwestern borders of North Carolina. During the past August, he and his men had been driven by the British leader, Patrick Ferguson, over the mountains to the Watauga settlement to seek safety. Talatu had heard all about it from Shinn. Now McDowell was coming back to his home here. It was at Quaker Meadows that the over-mountain troops would be joined by other groups to march once more against Ferguson.

Talatu thought scornfully, "They will be beaten again." The thought pleased him.

The boy watched as Shinn stored jerky and a wallet of cornmeal in the saddlebags and threw them across the horse's withers. He tied their blankets to the bags and climbed up and sat on the quilt that had been under the packsaddle. Shinn then reached down a hand to the Cricket and hauled him up to sit behind.

Kirk handed the rifle to the boy and said, "Fare thee well for the time being."

115

Shinn nodded to the two men and jerked on the reins, and Shucky set off at an easy lope.

"Find Ferguson so we can whittle him down to a point," Wells called after them.

They rode south along a dusty, rutted road, skirting a range of low hills. At the first house they came to, Shinn got down and went inside with his wallet of cornmeal.

This did not appear to be a dwelling to Talatu. There were no fields or barns around it. And on the wall was a wooden board on which was painted a deer and a bottle. What could it mean? His people painted religious symbols on their house posts and carved them on rocks. Were these religious signs of the unegas?

"Swapped my meal for journey cake in this here tavern," Shinn said when he returned. "And here's a noggin of perry cider for you."

The boy took the steaming cup and sipped. The liquid was sweet and strange. When he had downed it all, he felt considerably less weary, but a little dizzy.

While Shinn took the cup inside, the Cricket thought about this place the man had named "tavern." He saw now that the painted board on the wall meant "food and strange drink." When Cherokee traveled, they either took their food with them or killed it on the way, and they drank from springs. But unegas were too weak and lazy to travel in that fashion and had to have special houses to furnish them meat and drink.

Shinn climbed back on Shucky, and they rode south again.

They met many travelers, some pushing carts piled with possessions, a few on horseback, but most walking with light loads.

To everyone they met, Shinn called out a greeting and then reined in the horse. "Any news of the war, friend?" he asked.

"Cornwallis and his red-coated devils are heading for Charlotte," one man replied. "Our army's gone home, and I reckon nothing can stop the British from marching right on up to Phillydelphia."

"What do you hear about Ferguson?" Shinn inquired.

"He's around doing meanness, for that's his nature," the traveler told him. "But where he's at, I ain't heard nobody say."

Shinn and the boy rode on. No one Shinn questioned that afternoon knew anything of Ferguson's movements. Shinn muttered and shook his head. Talatu did not see how you could lose sight of an army. Cherokee warriors always knew where their enemies were. But then the white skins' peaceful ways were peculiar enough, so their warring ones were sure to be the same.

Sometimes a traveler would glare at the two on horseback and pass without a word. Others did not reply to Shinn's question but asked instead, "How come you hauling that there savage around?"

Shinn would laugh and answer something like,

"Oh, he's got a frumulated brain and a sizzled gullet and I'm taking him home to be cured," and then ride away fast.

"You pay no attention to what I say," Shinn told Talatu. "Folks want an answer to a question. They don't care what kind."

Once a whole family approached along the road, a man, followed by a woman, then five children strung out one behind the other. The woman carried a skillet, but the rest were empty-handed.

"Any news of the war, sir?" Shinn asked.

"The news is that the British done took everything I got in this wide world." The man scowled. "I told them me and my family were Loyalist and on their side, but they just laughed and drove away all my cows, killed my pigs and chickens, and burned down my cabin."

He passed the riders, and Shinn spoke politely to each of the others. Their faces were grimy and their clothes patched-together rags. Talatu could see that they wondered about him, how he came to be dressed in good breeches and a shirt and was carrying a fine rifle.

From up the road the father called back, "Damn the British king!"

Talatu's legs began to ache from riding astraddle. He shifted to ride sidewise, but it was no help. He longed to get down and walk, but Shinn was in a hurry. By and by Shucky's rocking lope made Talatu sick. But he was too proud to beg Shinn to stop.

The road turned into scattered low hills and followed alongside a stream.

"You keep a lookout behind," Shinn told him. "Anybody could come out of these woods and sneak up behind."

Talatu was too stiff and sore to turn around. He rocked and swayed and held tight to Shinn. The hills flattened and the roadway forked. Shinn stopped, unsure which road to take. Though it was late afternoon, there was still light to travel by. They must go on as far as they could before camping, he said.

The man chose the road that appeared to be the most traveled. At sunset they left the road to camp in a little thicket of trees. Talatu ate his smoked meat and bread in silence. His bones ached and throbbed. He knew his legs would never be the same again. He dreaded getting up the next day and riding Shucky.

Shinn roused him before daylight. Talatu got out of his blanket slowly. He was so stiff that he could hardly stand. In the nearby stream he waded out until the water reached his waist. He said a quick prayer to the Long Person, then splashed water over his face and body. The water was bitter cold, and it made his skin tingle and his blood race. He got out and rubbed his legs until the aching muscles eased a little. Still, he hated to climb back on Shucky.

He would have liked to comb and rebraid his hair, but there was no time.

They set off in the predawn darkness. Shinn did not push as hard as on the preceding day. Most of the time Shucky went at a walk. Shinn sang one sad song after another. Talatu wished he would not sing.

He opened his mouth to ask if he might be allowed to walk beside the horse when off in the distance he spied a group of horsemen through an opening in the oak woods. He pointed them out to Shinn.

"Loyalist, I'll wager, doing a bit of raiding," the unega told him. "I don't aim to tangle with 'em." He put Shucky into a lope, and they were soon out of sight of the horsemen.

They met only two travelers during the morning, both of whom passed in silence. There were more farms along the way than there had been on the day before—prosperous-looking, with cattle around the barns and haystacks and shocks of corn in the fields. Shinn said the owners were likely Tories who had been spared Ferguson's raids because of their British sympathies.

The sky was clear and the day hot. The boy welcomed a stretch of road where tree limbs stretched overhead and the way was cool and shady.

Suddenly, back among the trees to one side, something crashed through the undergrowth. Shinn reined to a halt. A man on horseback burst from the woods onto the road and wheeled to face Shinn. He wore a torn coat and a broad-brimmed hat turned up into three corners. A pistol was in his belt, and a sword hung at his side.

Four others rode onto the road and reined in behind their leader. They were all armed with pistols or muskets, and some had live fowls tied to their saddles. Behind one, a small gutted pig dripped blood from its slit throat.

"Morning," greeted Shinn. His voice was pleasant and easy, but Talatu could feel the tenseness, even fear, in his back muscles.

For a moment none of the newcomers answered. They sat silently staring, and the Cricket saw they did not know what to make of a white man and an Indian boy here on the roadway.

At last the leader asked, "Where you off to so early?"

"Oh, me and the boy here figured we might offer our services to Ferguson," Shinn replied. "It may be he can use two scouts. But we can't seem to find hide nor hair of him."

The first man snickered. "A dirty heathen boy— ain't that something," he exclaimed. "Major Ferguson won't be pleased to have such in his army."

"He's a fine shot with a rifle," interrupted Shinn. "Ain't nobody better than him at slipping up on folks—quiet as a snake."

"Where you from?" the leader asked. "You don't look to be from these parts."

"Up country a ways," Shinn said lightly. "Around Salisbury."

Again there was the sound of a horse coming through the woods. A lone rider shot out of the trees and pulled up beside the others.

"Wouldn't wait for me, would you?" he said in an

accusing voice. He pointed to a sack tied to his saddle. "Well, I ain't sharing none of this silver truck with you."

Talatu's heart formed into a cold, hard lump in his chest. The newcomer was Tyce. Shinn turned his head and said in a low voice, "Be ready to get out of here fast."

Then Tyce turned and saw them. A hasty grin stretched across his face. He turned to the first man. "How come you're speaking so polite to a coward and a savage? Dirty traitors. Don't you know these two is from over-mountain country? From Watauga?"

And Shinn answered, "Why, it's Felty Tyce, a varmint so lowdown snakes won't talk to him. Usually he rides a goat—horses can't stand the smell."

"Don't you call me no names, Shinn," snarled Tyce.

"And where are your Tory friends, Crawford and Chambers?" Shinn asked levelly.

"Oh, they're with Ferguson telling him all about the over-mountain army," Tyce replied. "But I figured I'd be more help riding about the country. Folks are mighty generous here. They been giving me silver and cattle and fine clothes."

He kicked his horse in the sides and rode toward them, pulling a pistol from his belt. Halting beside them, he glared at Talatu. "Don't you try to raise that rifle and shoot me," he growled. "Else I'll kill you first and my friends yonder will finish off Shinn."

He cocked the pistol with a great flourish. Slowly he raised the weapon until it pointed straight at Shinn's head. It was easy to see that Tyce enjoyed every moment of this. His riding friends also.

The Cricket was frightened. He trembled so much that he could barely hold on to the rifle lying across his legs. The butt of the gun was toward Tyce. Talatu knew he would never be able to swing the barrel up and around toward the man without being shot first.

No wonder Shinn had sung his doleful songs. He must have known that his mission was more dangerous than he had told the Cricket. He must have suspected that before the day was over, his life-path and Talatu's would come to an end.

Chapter 16

TALATU held his breath as he watched Tyce's finger tighten and tighten on the trigger. Shinn waited, silent and unmoving. The Cricket thought that he could shove Shinn from the horse into Tyce's arm and gallop away on Shucky. It was a mad thought and went in and out of his brain like a mouse darting among grasses.

Suddenly he was aware of the talisman hanging inside his shirt. It felt heavy and hot, and its power spoke to him. He listened and was reminded of the battle cry of Old Coat when death threatened his war party.

"Be brave!" he would call out to his warriors. "The earth is all that lasts forever—it is a good day to die! Aiiii-yiiii! Fight!"

Talatu knew what must be done and that he must act boldly and at once. With one quick motion he slid the rifle across his legs and slammed the butt into the muzzle of Tyce's horse.

The animal screamed in pain and reared, throwing Tyce backward. The pistol exploded into the air.

Shinn swung Shucky in front of the other horse,

and they rushed headlong through the trees. Shouts and shots rang out behind them, and the Cricket thought, "I am the one who will be struck." He could almost feel the impact of the lead ball in his back, but it did not come, and they galloped on. Limbs raked across their faces and shrubs and vines tore at their legs. Talatu clutched the rifle and clutched Shinn and wondered how much longer he could hold on.

They came out of the woods and raced up a slope, careening among tree stumps. At the crest Shucky paused, and the boy glanced back. He could not see anyone. They went down the other side of the hill and at the bottom came to a swamp. Shinn rode straight into the black water among the reeds and broken trees. Shucky had trouble lifting his legs. Each hoof sucked out of the clinging muck with effort.

Then they reached a small stand of cane and firmer ground, and Shinn halted. The horse stood with heaving sides and drooping head. Talatu's heart beat wildly, and still he grasped Shinn's waist with a frantic fist. Shinn loosened his grip gently and sat listening.

"You was clever," he told the boy. "I didn't have no notion how we was going to get out of that."

They waited. Strings of bubbles rose to the swamp's surface and burst with little popping noises. Back in the dimness, Talatu saw something moving. It was only a bog heron. The bird flew overhead with a hoarse croak.

Then they heard the far-off sound of horses and men's voices. The noises descended the hill toward the swamp.

"They're not here," someone called out.

"In the swamp maybe." Talatu recognized Tyce.

"Maybe so, but I ain't going in," the first man said. "Bad in there."

"It ain't big," Tyce argued. "We'll divide and ride around it."

There was a little more argument. Eventually they seemed to follow Tyce's plan. A few went one way, the rest another. When they were gone, Shinn quickly turned Shucky about and headed back to the spot where they had entered the swamp. He urged the horse and prodded him, and soon they were back on land. Shinn sat looking and listening. No one was in sight, and Shinn set the horse into a lope.

Fields flashed by, then woods, again and again as they pounded along. Talatu dared not turn his head. He only hung on and waited to die. They came to a path, and Shinn slowed the animal to a walk. Shucky was tiring and blowing hard. All at once they were among a great number of horses, tethered among the trees. Some grazed on clumps of grass, others fed from nosebags. There were several carts and wagons gathered in front of a house, not a log cabin, a house of boards. It looked strange to Talatu.

Shinn leaped to the ground. "Hide the rifle and all our gear over yonder under that down tree," he told the boy. "Hurry!"

Talatu did as he was told. Shinn was hastily rubbing the foam and sweat and mud from Shucky's
sides and legs with wads of grass. He tied the horse
between two others.

Grabbing the boy by the hand, Shinn pulled him
across the clearing and up to the entrance of the
house. Had Shinn lost his wits, the Cricket wondered. They would be trapped inside with no chance
to run if Tyce should come in after them.

Shinn eased open the door, and it squeaked loudly.
Talatu saw rows of men and women with their backs
to them, but not one glanced around at the sound of
the door. The two of them stepped inside.

What was this gathering, puzzled the boy? Women
in cloaks and bonnets sat on one side on backless
benches, men in dark coats and wide-brimmed hats
on the other. No one moved, and Talatu had the
strange feeling they might all be dead.

Why had Shinn come inside? There was no place
to hide among these motionless people. Then Shinn
began towing him toward the women's side over
against the wall where there was a space on a bench
for them.

"He is mad," thought the Cricket.

Next to him sat a large woman in a brown shawl
and beyond her a girl not much older than Talatu.
Still no one moved or glanced in their direction. It
was deadly quiet.

From outside a voice called, "Reckon they went on,
Tyce. No sign of them here."

"I'll look inside just in chance," Tyce replied.

Shinn leaned across Talatu, touched the large woman's arm, and whispered to her. She stared for a long space and swiftly took her shawl and handed it to the man. Quickly she removed the bonnet from the girl's head, at the same time pulling the child's neckerchief over her hair. Without surprise, the girl smoothed it and retied it.

The woman crammed the bonnet on Talatu's head and tucked his braids out of sight. Now he and Shinn were women among women.

Talatu tensed as the door squeaked loudly again. Would Tyce think to peer among the benches at the feet and legs of the congregation? The woman put her arm around his shoulder as though calming a restless child.

There was a booted step on the bare floorboards, then another. Talatu shrank closer to the large-bodied woman, glad for her protection. No one turned to look at the newcomer. The silence stretched and stretched, and still Tyce stood there. The Cricket had to make himself keep his eyes fastened on the backs of the women before him. He wanted to look around toward the door and see why Tyce took so long. Had he seen the two escapees?

Then the boots clomped out, and the door squeaked. "Quakers beat me," Tyce said loudly to his companions. "Silly folk a-setting there so proud with their hats on."

The words echoed in the still room.

"We done spent enough time on this goose chase," a man said. "We lost 'em. Let's get back."

There was a pause. "All right, but I ain't done with Shinn yet," Tyce answered.

As the horsemen rode off, a man at the front of the group stood and removed his hat and began to speak. Talatu could not follow his words. The man sat down, and a woman sitting on a stool turned to face the wall and began to read from a book in a singsong voice.

Shinn handed the shawl back to the woman with a whispered thanks, and the boy gave her the bonnet. She nodded at them as they rose. Outside, at the far side of the clearing, the horsemen were disappearing into the trees.

That night at their campfire Shinn told the boy that Quakers took their hats off only when speaking to God and explained other Quaker beliefs. Talatu listened closely in spite of his weariness. He had been impressed. The way that white woman had helped to save them, strangers, had struck him deeply. He went to sleep as soon as he had downed the last of their jerky.

For the next few days they traveled on, slowly and cautiously. Food was hard to come by. Many times they went hungry. Once, while Shinn scouted about the country, the Cricket hid in a canebrake. A raccoon came visiting him, and he shot it. It was not as tasty as venison, but it was food.

Shinn left the boy alone often as he rode about the

region seeking Ferguson's trail. Then one day he returned and said the British leader had gathered his scattered forces and headed east toward Kings Mountain.

Shinn and Talatu had been moving southward. Now they too turned toward the east, crossed the Broad River, and at dusk the following day discovered the British camp. Climbing a small hill, they lay overlooking the tents and cooking fires.

It was as noisy as the gathering at Sycamore Shoals, but the soldiers were dressed in more colorful clothes than the drab over-mountain men. Talatu watched a squad of red-coated soldiers march through the camp, and he wondered how they managed to fight with so much equipment on their backs. Cherokee warriors traveled light and could maneuver through the woods easily. But those soldiers with their stiff gait and their heavy packs would never be able to do that. Though the British were staunch friends, the boy doubted the Canoe would allow such soldiers to join him on a raid.

Off to one side was a tent, and on poles before the entrance several flags floated in darkening air. A red-coated soldier marched back and forth in front of the tent, his gun on his shoulder. At the end of the musket gleamed a long metal blade. The British tied their knives to their guns. They were mad, Talatu thought.

"A bayonet," Shinn explained when asked. "You

get close enough with one of them, you can run a man through."

Talatu rolled up in his blanket early but had trouble getting to sleep, for he was hungry. Shinn continued to watch the camp.

The following morning the noise of the army leaving woke them. It was still dark. Shinn took a quick look and said on his return, "They're leaving mighty early. Scared, I reckon. We'll move along with 'em, but off in the woods a ways, out of sight."

He threw the saddlebags on the horse and added, "Wish we had a mite to eat. I'm so hungry I could eat a log cabin, chinking, chimley, and all." He laughed.

Talatu said nothing. Indians could stand hunger better than weak white skins. Still, he would have liked food before he began another day of riding.

They made their way down the slope and struck out across the fields. At the edge of a thicket they came on two men cooking. The men did not look like British soldiers to the boy, but he did not care who they were, they had food. One man tended to spitted fowls roasting over the fire, while the other poked inside a steaming pot. "These potatoes are done," he said suddenly.

Shinn urged Shucky slowly forward. "Then share a bit," he said.

The men looked up, startled.

"Be worth our lives to do it," said one. "Major Ferguson will be wanting all of this and more when we get it to him. Couldn't wait for his breakfast and went ahead, and said we'd best not tarry over it."

The other cook said, "Be off!" He started toward a wagon to one side. On the seat lay a musket and a pistol.

Casually Shinn took the rifle from Talatu and pointed it at the man. "Let those weapons be," he said. "And I reckon the major had rather share with us than lose two good cooks."

The cooks appeared alarmed, but they were no more shocked than Talatu himself. Had he misunderstood the words? He could scarcely believe what Shinn had said. Kill two white men! What had happened to the man's beliefs?

"Cricket," Shinn said evenly. "Slide down and get us a couple of them birds and some taters. We won't take more than we can use, and I expect the farmer that got robbed of this food had rather see us eat it than that fancy major in his coat and ruffles."

Talatu was on the ground and walking toward the cooking fire before he remembered that the rifle was not loaded. The two cooks could run him through with the knives lying on a rock by the fire. Shinn could not defend him. He could not defend himself. The Cricket was frightened. He tried to keep his face and eyes from revealing his thoughts and fears. How could Shinn be so cool and sure?

Keeping his eyes on the cooks, the boy took two chickens and several potatoes and stuffed them into the saddlebag. Then he quickly climbed back on

Shucky, and Shinn spurred the horse forward past the men, faster and faster until the trees hid them.

In a sheltered cove Shinn reined to a stop, and they ate the hot fowls and potatoes. Talatu thought food had never tasted so good.

"Rifle not loaded," Talatu said as he crunched on a bone. "Might kill me—you."

"Well, them two didn't know the rifle wasn't primed." Shinn grinned. "If they'd come at you, we'd just have had to skedaddle, hell-for-leather. And we'd be powerful hungry. So I'm pleased you braved it out. I'll have to admit I was a mite uneasy."

They had both been brave, but they had both been foolish. How much better it would have been to have the rifle loaded and ready to shoot.

But the boy had to admit Old Coat had been right. Shinn was a man of peace, and the Cricket somewhere inside himself admired the man.

Chapter 17

THE FOOD Shinn had commandeered had been good, but by afternoon Talatu was again hungry. He was weary, too. He hated to think that Shinn seemed tougher than he, that the long day of riding and walking as they played this foolish game of spying did not seem to affect the white man as it did him.

Perhaps white people often spent their days peering down from hillsides at camps of soldiers, creeping close to hear what the British and the Loyalists were saying. Perhaps they were used to it.

Talatu, kneeling by Shinn and staring over the top of a log, saw only one thing that impressed him—an officer in a bright red coat and gold braid and plumed hat. There was a shiny sword at his side. His uncles and Dragging Canoe had done well to choose the side of those who were so proud and fine.

Shinn backed away from the log, and the Cricket went with him. Getting to his feet, he stumbled and fell. He thought the noise would bring the soldiers, but no one seemed to notice. Shinn helped him to the spot where they had hidden the horse.

"You ain't no cricket now," he remarked. "You

look more like a chick with the pip. I wish I hadn't had to fetch you with me. You'll be down with the pleurisy again. And it's coming on to storm."

He sighed. "Troubles. But at least we've done what we was told to do," he said, rubbing his chin. "I know for sure Ferguson ain't setting out for Charlotte. He aims to draw up his lines on top of Kings Mountain. Now all we got to do is get that news to Sevier and the over-mountain militia."

They began to walk, leading Shucky, and found an old path, grown up in briers and sumac. Crossing a stream, they came on a cabin, a tumbledown, caved-in house with a little tree poking through the broken roof and moss growing on the logs.

"We'll hole up here, while I scout around for somebody to ride back with my information," Shinn said. "Shucky's too wore out to get us back anyway."

He hobbled the horse and went inside. "Chimley's still all right," he pointed out, "and the walls and roof look pretty good at that end."

It was so. It would give sufficient shelter, the boy saw.

"You stay here and get a fire going," he said. "I'll be back afore dark. We can have a fire, even if we can't have no supper, and a place to sleep out of the wet."

He was gone out the door, and his footsteps faded swiftly. Talatu was tired and confused. All he could think was that the man was leaving him here and likely not coming back. He was panic-stricken suddenly. Shinn had left him here among enemies and strangers.

He ran outside and gazed down the path, but there was no sign of Shinn. He did not want Shinn to go. He needed the man more than ever now that he was farther from home than he had dreamed of being.

He splashed across the creek and ran blindly. Then he slowed, afraid that he was lost and would never catch Shinn. But luck was with him. He recognized a lightning-struck tree, a pile of rocks, a tall and flaming maple sapling. He was running toward the British camp. He turned aside quickly.

Suddenly he scrambled through some thin undergrowth, and there was Shinn—only an arrow-shot down the road, standing beside a wagon and talking to another white man.

It was a relief to find him. Shinn had not deserted him, and the boy was ashamed of not having stayed at the cabin. He would wait here and return with Shinn.

Shadow stretched along the roadway and lay deep on each side. But a movement caught Talatu's eyes at once, and he saw the figure in greasy buckskins slipping away from the British camp and through the trees.

It was Tyce! Shinn had been careless and let Tyce see him there in the middle of the track in plain view. Talatu watched Tyce slide from shadow to shadow. He had a rifle. He would shoot Shinn. Neither of the two other white men noticed. They were talking earnestly, in easy range of Tyce's bullet.

Tyce stopped and raised the rifle. Talatu's knees almost buckled under him. The man was going to shoot the boy's only hope of ever returning to Chota. If Shinn was killed, the boy's own death was assured. Suddenly he could stand it no longer and stepped onto the road.

"Shinn!" he yelled. "Tyce behind you!"

At once Shinn swung himself up into the wagon. The other man picked up the reins and started to turn the horses, crouching low as he did so.

Talatu could see that Shinn was going to escape. He was down in the wagon on his knees and gave Tyce little to shoot at. Then Tyce turned the rifle toward Talatu and screamed, "Your little savage, Shinn—I'll kill him!"

Talatu had forgotten his own danger. He had forgotten that Tyce had always hated him and had tried to kill him before. It would be an easy shot. Even if the Cricket turned to run, the bushes were so thin that he would have no protection.

What happened next happened so quickly that Talatu could not be sure of it. He heard the wagon creak and saw the wild, frightened looks of the two horses and the standing, swaying figure of Shinn, tomahawk in hand.

Tyce saw Shinn, too, and swung his rifle toward him and pulled the trigger. There was a flash and smoke, and at the same time there was the gleam of the tomahawk tumbling through the air. The boy saw it go cleanly into the front of Tyce's skull. The man staggered and turned a blood-streaked and astonished face to the sky as he fell.

The wagon rolled on, but there was only one passenger, for Shinn lay on the ground, unmoving.

Chapter 18

TALATU stood in the dusty road, staring at the dark red pool that spread wider and wider around Shinn. The shock he felt was as strong as if he had been the one struck by a bullet.

Then the boy roused himself. The soldiers in the British camp had heard the rifle shot. They would be coming to investigate. He must get Shinn away at once. He turned the man over and tried to get a firm hold under his arms. He would drag him into the undergrowth if he could do it by himself. When he heard the wagon returning, he was grateful. Surely the driver would help.

"Had trouble quieting the horses," the wagoner explained as he jumped down. Together they lifted Shinn into the back of the vehicle. "I can take him to my house," the driver said, picking up the reins. "But it's a mite dangerous."

Talatu wanted no more of strangers, no more of white people, even if this one was a friend of Shinn.

"No." He spoke quickly. "We got a place. Take Shinn there."

As they rolled off into the trees, Talatu gave Tyce

one last disdainful glance. Then he pointed out the trail. The horses had a difficult time pulling through the underbrush, but at last they were at the abandoned house and laid Shinn inside on the floor.

Shinn's eyes were closed, and his breath was harsh and uneven. The front of his shirt was soggy with blood. The driver slit open Shinn's shirt. Talatu flinched when he saw the ugly wound oozing blood.

The wagoner whistled and shook his head. "A chest wound that bad, a man ain't got much chance to live," he said in a low voice. "If'n he dies, it'll be because he wanted to save your life."

Talatu did not answer.

"He could of got away, but he stood up and threw that tomahawk to save you," the man continued. "I reckon he sure thinks a heap of you."

Still Talatu said nothing. The wonder stone burned against his chest. If Shinn died, Talatu knew he had lost more than his life in saving the Cricket. To save him, Shinn had murdered another man. It was a double death, for Shinn had also sacrificed his beliefs. Talatu understood that with his whole being. Shinn had done a brave and terrible thing, to go against his own gods, peculiar as they might be.

"Shinn was always a strange one," the wagoner remarked. "But he was good. Always fair and honest."

The wounded man opened his eyes and looked at the two kneeling beside him. "Lusk," Shinn said weakly and then coughed. "This boy . . . Cricket

". . . I'm obliged if you . . . get him home . . . I may not . . . not . . ."

He seemed to slip again into unconsciousness. Lusk stood up, looking worried.

"I got to go," he told the boy. "I got a wife down with the ague fever. If'n he comes to, tell him he's got no cause to worry. I owe him a favor, and I'll see you get on a path home, maybe go partway with you. Ain't many white men care to travel it, rough as it is, and you'll be safe riding Shinn's horse and toting his rifle."

He brought a bucket from the wagon and promised to come back with food as soon as he could. Then the wagon squeaked off into the twilight.

Talatu brought water from the stream; then he made a fire. There was plenty of wood in the cabin, bits of the roof and even the walls and floor. He sat staring into the flames, trying not to hear Shinn's whistling, moaning breath.

The storm Shinn had predicted rushed down on the cabin—wind and lightning and thunder that shook the ground. It moved on, leaving a steady downpour of rain. The damp and chill of the night came in through the open door, and the boy was thankful that they had found a dry, warm spot.

"Water," the wounded man muttered.

Talatu soaked a piece of tow in the bucket and squeezed drops into Shinn's mouth until he turned away. Then he bathed the bearded face and wiped the blood from the wound. He shuddered all the while, but he kept his hand steady. He could do nothing except wait.

Once the unega turned his head toward the Cricket and said distinctly in Cherokee, "Oconee—no day has gone by that I did not long to see you."

Talatu was frightened. Had a spirit made the white man speak the language of the Real People and mention the boy's own mother's name? No, he reasoned, if Shinn had known Old Coat and Neeroree, he might easily have known Oconee. And Talatu remembered the times Shinn had spoken or understood Cherokee words before.

Shinn and Old Coat had not wanted the Cricket to find out that Shinn knew the language. It was part of the secret and the mystery between the two men. He piled more wood on the fire and stared down at the man's pale face. By and by Shinn asked again for water, and the boy gave it to him.

"You're a fine boy," said Shinn in a whisper. "Good boy . . . glad you come with me . . . to be my boy. . . ." He coughed, and a little blood ran from his lips. Talatu wiped it away.

A moment later Shinn spoke again in Cherokee. ". . . the Darkening Land . . . into the Darkening Land . . ." Once more Talatu was frightened. The shadowy land of death was so close that Shinn could see and feel it. Then Shinn's breathing grew a little easier, and for a while he slept.

Talatu squatted and wondered what was it that this

unega and Old Coat and Oconee knew that he did not?

At last Shinn opened his eyes and gasped, "Cricket!"

Talatu moved closer.

"I was a trader then." Shinn's hoarse words were slow. "And she was beautiful, your mother—and kind and good. I loved her. I love her yet. Things happened, and I had to leave." His strange light eyes moved back and forth, back and forth, looking for something. Suddenly they fastened on Talatu's eyes.

"Talatu . . . Cricket . . . my son," he finished.

The boy sprang to his feet. He was shocked and almost faint. But it was true! He knew it was true! It made everything clear, why Old Coat had sent him with this white man, why the man had come for him and wanted him to stay for a year, why his mother had agreed to his going. He knew it deep inside where his spirit dwelled, where his thoughts thronged in darkness.

He knew it as he knew his own name—this man was his father! A white man was his father! The blood of the hated and horrible unegas flowed in his veins.

He could scarcely breathe; it was all he could do to keep from running out into the rainy night, crying and cursing. How could Old Coat and his young uncles stand the sight of him? How could they?

After a minute he calmed a little. He was still his

mother's son, a member of the Wolf Clan. Nothing could take that away from him, no matter that he had mixed blood. A boy belonged to his mother and her clan and to her brothers. His father did not matter.

But to be half white! He writhed and twisted with the pain of it.

Shinn groaned. Talatu stared down at him. His father! His father! What a dreadful thing to be the son of this white-eyed, white-skinned enemy.

Yet Shinn was a good man. He had been kind always to the Cricket. And on this day he was dying a twofold dying—he had killed and so been killed in two ways, to save his son.

The Cricket squatted again and pondered and hoped and ached and feared. He tended the fire and watched the blood drip from Shinn's chest in a small stream. After a while the man cried out, "Oconee! Talatu!" His breathing grew harder and slower and slower, and then it ceased.

Shinn was dead.

Talatu was alone, terribly alone, and far from home among strangers and enemies. If the wagon driver did not return, he had no notion how to get back to Chota, how to avoid meeting white men who would kill him on sight. And Shinn was dead! Suddenly the Cricket burst into tears. He wept a long time and finally fell asleep by the body of his father.

When he awoke, the rain had stopped and white autumn mist lay everywhere in streaks and pools. A good day, Old Coat always said, for such fogs would lift quickly and mean fine weather later.

The Cricket could hear Shucky moving about outside the house. He must act swiftly before Lusk returned or anyone came near. Shinn lay by the dead fire with his strange eyes shut and his face closed, all his secrets still inside him. Oconee! Talatu's mother's name lingered in the cabin. He could hear it yet.

He would give Shinn a burial. He wanted to do it himself, not Lusk, should he return. Talatu would take his father to the stream nearby. The Long Person was always helpful to the Cherokee and certainly would not object to helping a lone Cherokee boy in his time of sorrow. Shinn would approve, the Cricket was sure.

Wearing only his breechclout, he pulled the body from the cabin and through the wet grass to the stream. It was hard work. But he was determined and at last laid the dead man at the little river's edge. He weighted Shinn with stones and wished he had the man's hat in which to bury him. Shinn was hardly Shinn without that black, shapeless headgear. Talatu towed the body along in the water until the current seized it and pulled it down into a deep hole.

Standing waist deep in the stream he sang:

"You, Long Person,
With your head in the mountains and your feet in
the lowlands;

Helper of the Cherokee, you let nothing slip from
 your grasp.
Hold my father's body in your arms forever."

The words were his own and possibly not the right words. He was not a priest and did not know the proper ways to do such things. However, he did not believe the Long Person would be offended.

He returned to the cabin and slipped Old Coat's stone on its thong over his head and held it fast in his hands and prayed for wisdom and courage for himself and peace for the dead man. Then he dressed, and as he brought Shucky, his horse now, up to the door, he heard Lusk yelling at his horses as they splashed through the stream and up the muddy bank toward the cabin. The boy was relieved. The wagoner had kept his word.

He was going home. After all these months, he was going home. All his fine new possessions meant little compared to the joy of that thought.

And yet he was going home a different boy in every way from when he had left and with one horrible, hateful difference that would mark his whole life from now on.

The stone on his chest would help him. It would help him meet Old Coat's eyes with courage when he returned, knowing his great-uncle's secret, his mother's secret. It would help him go into the future bravely, no matter what it meant or where his life-path led.

Old Coat had loved him enough to give him his most precious talisman. Shinn had loved him enough to die for him and, somehow much worse for that strange man, to kill for him. Surely he owed his father and his great-uncle the duty of a strong heart and good thoughts and unstinting sacrifice, in the hope that he might bring about a little happiness and peace to those he lived among.

His blood might be two kinds, but his heart would be whole. He thought of Neeroree stirring over a pot of stew, of Old Coat warming his knees beside the fire, of Oconee laughing as she baked persimmon bread, and of his young uncles dancing and singing. Those he loved. He was going home.